Bibliographic information of the German National Library:
The German National Library lists this publication in the German
National Bibliography; detailed bibliographic data is available on the
internet through www.dnb.d-nb.de.

TWENTYSIX – The Self-Publishing-Publisher
A cooperation between the Publishing Group Random House and
BoD - Books on Demand.

Production and distribution by:
BoD – Books on Demand, Norderstedt

ISBN: 978-3-7407-0896-2

9 783740 708962

WALDO

CHARLEMAGNE'S PRIEST
742AD - 814AD

HISTORICAL FICTION
VOLUME I OF THE CHARLEMAGNE TRILOGY

KLAUS D WAGNER

Historical fiction.

This is a work of fiction. Characters, institutions, organisations or places including townships mentioned in this historical novel are either the product of the author's imagination or, if real, used fictitiously without any intention to describe actual conduct or events.

© 2016 Klaus D Wagner, Sydney Australia
Cover drawings: Roger McAuliffe
Page 6: Donatio Waldonis, Würzburg archives doco # 3220 Reg. 510. B
Page 7: The author Klaus D Wagner, private archive
Page 10: 'Circulus sive Liga Sveviae' by David Seltzlin 1572
English Language Editor: Roger McAuliffe

ISBN: 978-3-7407-0896-2

More about the book: www.the-charlemagne-trilogy.com

In Memoriam

Dedicated to Waldo, who, on June 11, 770AD, donated a church, which he built in Seeburg, to the Cloister Lorsch and who inspired me to write this historic novel.

About the Author

Klaus D Wagner was born on June 11, 1952 in Esslingen, Germany and grew up in a small Swabian town called Bad Urach.

After matriculation he studied marketing at the 'Stuttgart Media University' later working for an international advertising agency in Frankfurt.

In 1982 he immigrated to Sydney, Australia working in advertising on major accounts before establishing his own successful marketing business.

In 2001 he was awarded the 'Order of Merit' by the German Federal President.

He lives with his wife and two children in Sydney, Australia and in Bad Urach-Seeburg, Germany where this story originates.

Books by this author:

The Charlemagne Trilogy

I **Waldo** - Charlemagne's Priest
II **Godsbert** - Charlemagne's Scribe
III **Carolus** - Charlemagne's Life

Waldo

CHARLEMAGNE'S PRIEST
742AD - 814AD

Charlemagne's Christianisation of the pagans in the Dark
Ages of Medieval Europe was brutal enough.

It could have been far worse without Waldo, a more
considered Christian, by his side.

Historical fiction.
Volume I of The Charlemagne Trilogy

KLAUS D WAGNER

Donatio Waldonis

I am with God in Münsingen called Waldo and donate, as documented, for the wellbeing of my soul, and to the holy martyr Nazarius, who's body rests in Cloister Lorsch, where the abbot Gundeland is responsible in the name of Rome, that I shall always be present in the Alemannic area of Münsingen and Auingen, a church, farmland and meadows and also a church in the village of Trailfingen and another one in Seeburg.

Documented for Cloister Lorsch on June 11 in the second year of reign of King Charles. (Charlemagne - 770AD)

Klaus D Wagner

Epistolary

Dear Reader,

"Who was Waldo?" I hear you ask.

An original document, written in Latin on sheepskin in the early middle ages verifies the donation of a Christian church by a certain Waldo in Seeburg, a small village in Southern Germany.

No further historic records of this mysterious Waldo existed. I spent two years of intense research to unravel his alleged identity.

I concluded, that Waldo and Charlemagne, the mighty

Carolus Magnus were like the priest and the soldier, who shared a lifelong bond forged in childhood.

They saw themselves as Christianity's cross and sword, put on earth by God to build and defend Christendom in medieval Europe.

Both men differed in their approach to converting the pagans. Charlemagne, the soldier, believed in a swift decision and the beheading by sword of the unwilling: "My god is your god. My will be done."

Waldo, the priest, believed in a more gentle missionary way, bringing salvation with bread, wine and fear of the unknown, and the promise of a better life in heaven: "Jesus died for us on the cross for our redemption. Thy kingdom come. Amen!"

They also shared a terrible secret known only to themselves and God. It's a secret that history failed to uncover in the last 1250 years.

At this point I want to highlight and acknowledge the immeasurable help of my friend and editor Roger McAuliffe who turned my often clumsy thoughts and words into the refined writing befitting the Charlemagne Trilogy.

And those who read this book with an open mind, will hopefully care more about the authenticity of their spiritual experience than the historical authenticity of every chronicled aspect in this novel.

'Lege feliciter' as Waldo might have said in his Latin writing language meaning *'read happily',* he might have added a pious *'Amen'.*

Let me simply say: *'Enjoy!'*

Yours sincerely,

Klaus D Wagner

THE CHRISTIANISATION
OF THE PAGAN ALEMANNI

10

Posterity Quote

"You will never be forgotten in this place. As long as this fleeting world exists, your name will be endlessly praised, Waldo, oh thou most holy man."

Said the monks of St. Denis on Waldo's death in 814AD

Contents

Chapter	Title	Page
	In Memoriam	3
	Epistolary	7
	Posterity Quote	11
	Prologue	14
I	*Sword*	*21*
II	*Cross*	*24*
III	*Confession*	*27*
1	Arrival	30
2	Baptism	35
3	Love	39
4	Death	45
5	Refuge	51
6	Childhood	56
7	Schooling	64
8	Reunited	70
9	Ravenna	75
10	Agony	82
11	Bloodbath	86
12	Farewell	98

Chapter	Title	Page
13	Incarceration	106
14	Confrontation	111
15	Missionary	115
16	Symbols	124
17	Exams	128
18	Enlightenment	133
19	Ordination	146
20	North	155
21	Rejection	175
22	Belief	183
23	Devotion	192
24	Funeral	201
25	Mission	213
26	Visit	217
27	Donation	236
28	South	247
29	Sin	263
Epilogue		270
Postscript		281
Epiphany		283

Paul the Apostle was in a hurry. Ever since he had a vision of the resurrected Jesus Christ on the road to Damascus, he feared that the Armageddon, the end of the world, was near.

His mission was to convert as many Jews and Gentiles to his new faith of Christianity as possible. He preached that only the true believers in Jesus the Son of God and a descendant of King David were destined for heaven, all others were doomed to the fires of hell for eternity.

He and his companions undertook many missionary journeys and eventually sailed for Rome, Spain and Britain before returning to Jerusalem where he was arrested and martyred.

This need for urgency, for fear of the end of the world, persisted throughout the Early Middle Ages in Europe during the Merovingian and the Carolingian Dynasties.

The Merovingian royal family took its name from the renowned, almost legendary, King Merovech. He was succeeded by his son King Childeric. When Childeric died at Tournai in Belgium around 481 AD, his son Clovis acceded to the throne and the Franks emerged from obscurity.

Their history was recorded by a Gallo-Roman aristocrat, George Florentius, better known by his ecclesiastical name of Gregory, bishop of Tours. King Clovis proved to be a bloodthirsty young ruler, but despite that, Gregory admired his courage and tenacity and lauded him as the first Catholic king of the Franks.

In the 7th century, the wealth and influence of the Merovingian dynasty rapidly diminished, due to the growing power of the noble families. By the 8th century it had all but dried up and the Merovingian kings were rulers in title only.

Charlemagne's friend and biographer, Einhard, summed up the position of the last descendants of Clovis in colourful terms: "The king had nothing left but the enjoyment of his title and the satisfaction of sitting on his throne, his hair long and his beard trailing, acting the part of a ruler."

In the early 8th century, while Spain was succumbing to Muslim armies, Charles Martel, 'The Hammer', emerged. When the Muslims invaded Frankish lands Charles drove them out and finally ended Muslim expansion in Western Europe. The Frankish empire then came under the rule of the Carolingian dynasty, named after Charles – 'Carolus'.

Charles Martel was succeeded by his sons, Pippin and Karlman. Karlman eventually retired to St Benedict's monastery of Monte Cassino and Pippin became sole ruler of Francia. His father, Charles Martel, never called himself king, but Pippin wasn't so reluctant. In 754, he was anointed King of the Franks by Pope Stephen II.

When Pippin died in 768, his kingdom was divided between his two sons, Charles (Charlemagne) and Carloman.

The two brothers were in constant conflict, but in 771, at the age of only 21, Carloman died after a long illness, and conveniently for Charlemagne who took over as sole ruler of the Frankish empire.

†

Charlemagne was unrelenting, and often brutal, in his determination to convert Europe, the Frankish Empire, to Christianity and protect Christendom at all costs. And like Paul the Apostle, Charlemagne was in a hurry too.

The Carolingian dynasty saw Christianity as not only a means of salvation and the forgiveness of sins, but also as a tool to unite the people of the vast Empire and give them a feeling of national solidarity and belonging.

So, there were two powers at play, the Roman Catholic Church, which supported an apostolic conversion of the pagans, and the Frankish Kings, who wanted a much faster conversion.

The Church sent out missionaries to convert the pagan villagers through the power of the cross, by preaching Jesus Christ's message of the forgiveness of sins and a life to come in God's kingdom of heaven.

This apostolic approach was far too slow for the Carolingian kings. So they sent in their troops with swords and orders to kill all local noblemen who were not converting to Christianity as they were hindering the amalgamation of the Frankish Empire.

Two cruel historic events vividly illustrate the fierce determination of the Frankish kings to convert the pagans at all costs.

At the Bloodcourt of Cannstatt in 746AD, hundreds of helpless Suebi noblemen were killed by Charlemagne's uncle, King Karlman.

27 years later, in 773AD, Charlemagne killed thousands of Saxon prisoners of war for not obeying his orders to convert to Christianity .

Eventually the empire was converted to Christianity, and the Pope in Rome, with the help of the Frankish Kings, eventually became the powerful guardian of the unified Christian kingdom of the Carolingians.

†

The story that unfolds here in this book, begins in the middle of the 8th century, with Waldo, the missionary priest from the Cloister of Reichenau.

Taught and inspired by Irish-Scottish Monks, he sets out to convert the last bastion of the Frankish kingdom's barbaric pagans to Christianity, with nothing more than a cross, faith in God, and his own strength and courage.

His childhood friend, and King of the Franks, Charles the Great, also known as Charlemagne, pushes him to be less apostolic and more ferocious in his approach, explaining that the only power in a cross is the fear of the sword.

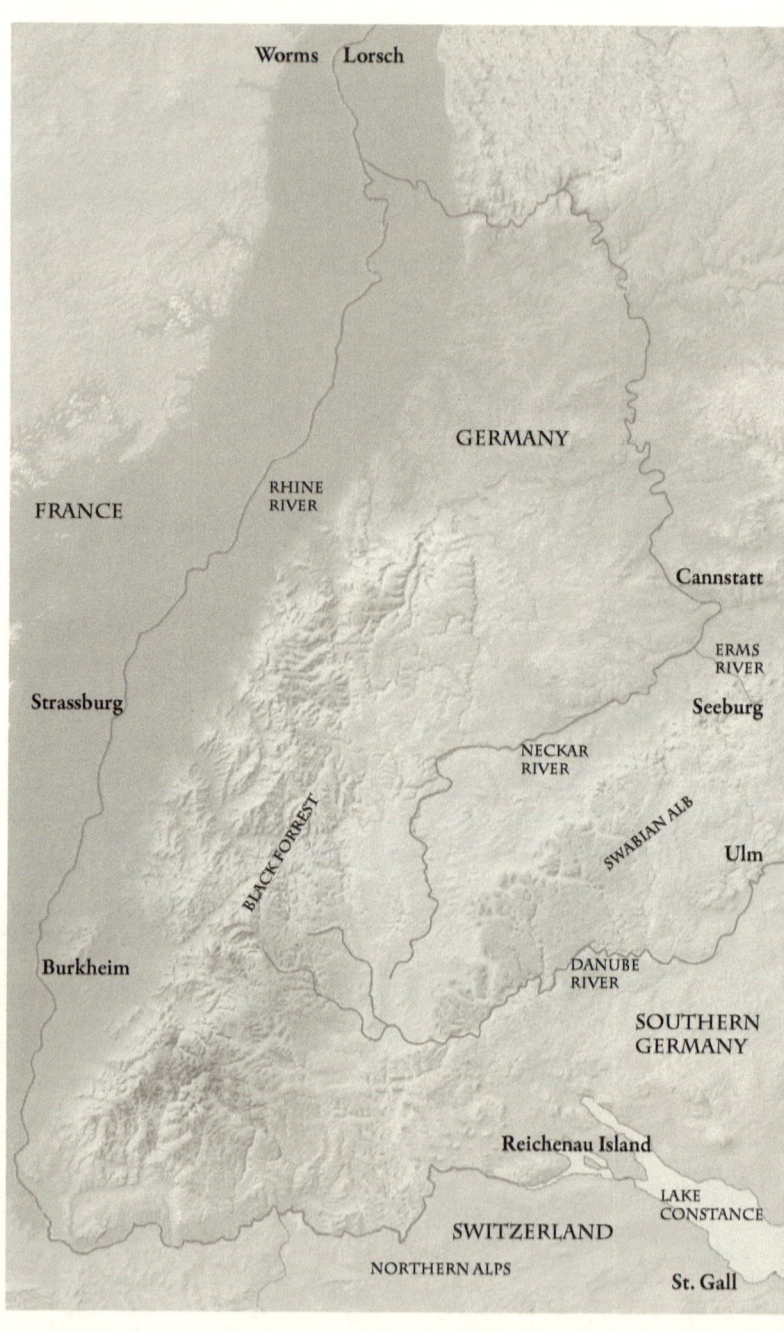

Abbey of St. Gall, December 6, 770AD

I

Sword

The moonlight floated to earth as a shimmering silver mist, illuminating the winter's night. It bathed the landscape in a pale glow, betraying the nocturnal predators lurking in their hidden places.

A great eagle owl dropped from its moonlit perch without a whisper of sound to find a darker place to hunt. As it glided low across the ground towards the forest, its gleaming blood orange eyes caught a glimpse of a tall, imposing figure silhouetted against the purple sky.

The great owl had seen this majestic man before, but never alone like this. There were always protectors. Where were they now? As powerful as he was, he had too many enemies to be wandering alone in the shadow time of the gathering dark.

Even here, in his own land, there were savage barbarians waiting for the black of night to spill the blood of Christian conquerors like him. Worse still, there were traitors whose loyalty could be bought for silver and gold. And there were murderous assassins who would slit this warrior's throat simply for the glory of their god.

He always had protectors, who would lay down their own lives to save his. But now there were none to be seen as he walked slowly, head bowed, as if in contemplation ... or penitence. He stopped and looked up ahead, and then behind, the way he had come, as if he might turn and go back to the safety of his protectors. Or perhaps it was to make sure he wasn't being followed. He turned forward again and his shoulders lifted as he sucked in a deep lungful of the cool night air.

His keen, bright eyes scanned the glowing landscape before him as he strode forward. Occasionally he peered deep into the shadows, made stronger and sharper-edged by the full moon, now partly obscured by the bell towers of the great abbey ahead of him in the distance.

The path he was following was taking him up hill to the abbey's gate. It ran along a narrow ridge, with the forest pressing in on both sides just a little way below him. As he moved forward once again, a bloodcurdling scream pierced the silence. It came from close by in the trees to his right. He swung round to face the sound, drawing his sword in the same flowing movement.

The moonlight flashed a brilliant gold along the full length of the blade. He stood with the sword angled across his chest, his other hand on the dagger at his belt, and listened. The scream reached him again, but this time it was less violent. It sounded several more times – now just a squeal. Then, abruptly, it was choked off and its echo faded away in the wind. A bear killing a wild pig, he decided.

He listened a while longer to the restored silence. Then, satisfied there was no immediate threat, he wrapped his gilded blue cloak around him and continued along the path.

He moved at a brisk pace, but his gaze keenly followed the edge of the path on his left, as if retracing his steps, looking for something precious he had lost earlier. The object of his search suddenly appeared just ahead of him, easily seen in the bright moonlight. It was a small pile of white stones, which he quickly brushed aside retrieving the dark bundle of wrapped cloth underneath. He vigorously shook it loose, held it up, and smiled.

A perfect fit, he thought. He put the garment on over his own clothing and pulled the cowl over his head. The magnificent abbey loomed above him, an awe-inspiring shape against the night sky.

He stood and admired its vast, brooding magnificence for several moments before striding forward once again, now as a monk not a king. A short time later he stopped again and looked behind him one last time, before leaving the path and melting into the night as the shadow of the abbey claimed him.

II

Cross

On the other side of the abbey wall appeared a second figure flitting in and out of the shadows as he strode purposefully towards the vast building towering over him.

The small metal cross hanging around his neck was of a dull lustre and not designed to impress or intimidate. Despite his humble attire however, this man was no stranger to the trappings of power.

He too heard the scream in the night, but it was a way off and he was accustomed to such sounds. He had no fear of wild beasts. Only the fear of God filled his heart. If the Lord wanted him to be devoured by wolves, then so be it.

This part of the northern Alps, he reflected, was beautiful and spectacular in the daylight, but now, at night, even under a bright moon, it could seem savage and frightening with its prowling predators and Godless Barbarians. But much more than that, it was also awe-inspiring and terrifying for another reason.

He knew that one might meet devils and run the risk of losing one's soul in this place, but one might also meet the Almighty. For all his holiness and devotion to his Creator, he wasn't ready to meet him.

Not tonight, at least. Tonight he had a duty to an earthly lord that he alone among men could perform.

With such thoughts urging him to greater exertion, he finally entered the abbey from a hidden rear entrance. Minutes later, he reached a side door to the church. The door opened onto three stone steps that took him straight up into the sacristy.

He replaced his humble monk's habit with his fine priest's vestments and climbed five more stone steps to the first floor. He hurried along a vaulted corridor running along the side of the nave, past a row of emblazoned shields and flickering candles hanging overhead.

As he reached the narthex he stepped directly into the chapel. The high rectangular windows faced south, away from the full moon in the eastern sky, so only the faintest glow of light reached them, shrouding the chapel in a soft grey gloom.

Along one wall were three bronze latticed doors, each opening into confessional recesses. Each confessional recess was made up of two narrow chambers with a small wooden mesh window between them. Under each window was a narrow shelf, and in each chamber a bench with a prayer book on it.

The priest lit the candle, closed the lattice door behind him and settled in the chair on one side of the gloomy confessional chamber. He sat motionless in the semi-darkness, head bowed in prayer, waiting for the most powerful and important man in the land to come and confess his sin. It was just one sin, but one he knew would be committed. A terrible sin he was obliged to forgive, and forget. Forgetting his own sin would be much more difficult.

III

Confession

The great sinner came through the front entrance and made his way briskly past the gatehouse, into the church hall and through to the narthex. From there he could see the altar at the far end of the nave, and to his left he saw that the door to the chapel was open.

He knelt on one knee, drew his sword and placed it firmly on the stone floor in front of him. Facing the altar, he bowed his head in prayer and remained that way for several minutes.

†

In the confessional chamber close by, all the priest heard was a sharp clink of sword on stone. A short time later he heard the sinner take his place at the other side of the mesh window.

The priest didn't bother to look up because there was nothing to see in the shadows behind the mesh, but he had a clear picture of the proud, regal head there with its white mane, strong nose and large penetrating eyes.

The deep voice resonated through the confined chamber. "Bless me father. Even a king must confess his sins."

"But not to everyone."

"To you only, my trusted Christian adviser, dear Waldo."

"Your sins are my sins, Charles."

"I plan to kill my brother. God forgive me!"

"First you will need Bertrada to forgive you."

"She will not, she is his mother too."

"But God will forgive you?"

"God is merciful."

"And what mercy will you show to your brother?

"It is necessary to kill him to protect the Christian faith!"

"Even your own brother?"

"It has to be done ... before he kills me."

"Christ didn't kill." said Waldo, the confessional priest.

No further response came from the darkness at the other side of the mesh window. The long silence condensed like dew on Charles's conscience.

"Are you still there? Waldo, my brother."

"Would you kill me then too, Charles ... if it had to be done?"

"You are my soul brother. We are joined at the heart, you and I Waldo. It would be as stabbing myself in the heart. It will be my natural earthly brother I kill."

"I could forgive you, in the name of the Lord. But I cannot bless what you plan to do. I wear a cross, not a sword."

Charles laughed bitterly: "A cross is a sword, a sword is a cross. We are sword and cross together."

"Then it will be 'we' who kill him, Charles – you and me."

"My sins are your sins, Waldo."

Some 21 years earlier...

City of Worms, July 1, 741AD

1

Arrival

"It is our sins that separate us from God," said Chrodegang the Bishop-in-waiting of Metz.

"Amen," came the response from the priests and monks gathered around him.

"We are conceived in the iniquity of sin," one of the monks said. The Bishop raised his hands and lifted his eyes towards the church's vaulted ceiling, as the others bowed their heads.

"Let us pray," he said. "Lord, you raised up John the Baptist to prepare each of us for Christ. We are to repent and – "

"They come! They come!" shouted an unseen voice. Seconds later a small boy burst into the church and ran up to the Bishop.

"They come!" he shouted again, unable to contain his excitement.

One of the monks constrained and calmed the boy.

"Hush Ruthard," he said gently, "his Grace is praying."

With a remarkable display of willpower, the wide-eyed boy obeyed.

"They come!" he whispered, looking up desperately at the monk who had his arm wrapped firmly around the boy's shoulders. The bishop frowned severely at the boy, then turned away with a wide smile on his face and continued his interrupted prayer.

"We are to repent and be baptised for the remission of our sins through the holy faith of St John the Baptist, burning and shining lamp of the world. This is God's instruction."

He turned and smiled at the boy.

"Tomorrow we have a christening to celebrate the cleansing of the original sin from the soul of the infant Waldo, son of Richbold, Count of Wetterau ... and baby brother of young Ruthard."

The bishop ruffled the boy's hair.

"So, they come!" he said happily. "Thank you Ruthard for this joyous news. And we thank the Lord for their safe arrival. Now let us go and welcome our exalted visitors."

†

Exalted they were. This was indeed a gathering of the highest in the land. Nobles, abbots and bishops making the journey to the city of Worms on the river Rhine and its Cathedral to attend the baptism of Richbold's second son, Waldo. And the most august guests of all were the future King Pippin and his brother Karlman, sons of the legendary ruler Charles Martel 'The Hammer'. As well as being a future king, on this day, July 1st 741, Pippin was also to be godfather to the infant Waldo the next day. The two brothers had just returned from their sister Hiltrude's marriage to the Bavarian Duke Odillo in Passau, two week's journey from Worms.

"Our cherished sister Hiltrude is now the Duchess of Bavaria!" Pippin announced, as he greeted his dear friend Richbold.

"Hail to the Duchess of Bavaria," Richbold declared to the gathered throng.

"To the Duchess of Bavaria!" they sang out with one voice. "May God fill her heart with joy!"

"Thank you my friends," Pippin sang back with a beaming smile. He then thumped Richbold vigorously on the back and threw his arm around his shoulder.

"Wine for our great and honoured guests!" Richbold ordered. He need not have bothered for the wine was already being poured.

"Now everyone must hear about our journey from Passau," Pippin said, taking a large goblet of wine in both hands, as if he were a priest grasping a chalice. "Karlman and I travelled along the Danube to Ulm where we disembarked our barges. We wanted to cross the Swabian Alb as we had heard so many strange and terrible tales about the pagan barbarians living in those God-forsaken lands at the far edge of our empire."

"They were sub-human and uncivilized, we were told," said Karlman, "and were guilty of the most vile and inhuman acts imaginable."

The gathered guests were now listening intently, expecting to hear horrible stories of bloodthirsty devil worship and the gruesome sacrifice of innocent children.

"That is not so," Karlman said, disappointing everyone. "It is true they are a rough-looking people clothed in animal skins and coarse linen. But they are no more bloodthirsty than anyone else. They are just poor, ignorant and living in squalor."

"They are not organized," said Pippin. "They have no civil rules or systems. The villages stink. All manner of filth and waste is tossed into the alleyways, and stays there until it rots. These barbarian people get sick all the time."

"We cannot allow this to continue in our own lands," Karlman said. "Life is not worth living as these barbarians live, and we must change it. No-one in the empire we rule has to live like a barbarian."

All those gathered cheered mightily and drank heartily to the health and benevolence of Pippin and Karlman.

"Friends! Friends!" shouted Pippin, trying to calm them. "Let us thank my great friend Richbold for his hospitality. And let us not overindulge ourselves today, because tomorrow we must celebrate the holy baptism of my godson, the infant Waldo. And we must do so with great dignity and respect under the gaze of the Lord our God." The gathered guests, now calm and quiet, nodded their agreement.

"Then, afterwards," Pippin cried, "We can overindulge!"

2

Baptism

A new day emerged from the pink glow that gently washed across the eastern sky. The arriving light was only just touching the top of the church's bell tower, painting it with a rosy hue.

The western door of the cathedral was still in darkness, but an array of torches and candles illuminated the baptistery and there was already a bustle of activity. Preparation for Waldo's baptism began early.

With the rulers Pippin and Karlman on the guest list, nothing could be left to chance. Richbold's instructions were that everything must be ready two hours before the christening, which was set for midday.

At noon precisely the church bells rang out across the countryside announcing to one and all that the christening of Waldo, second son of Richbold, the Count of Wetterau, had begun.

Richbold, with Pippin and Karlman at his side, led the male guests and family members into the church, and the door was closed behind them.

They took their places in the pews as Chrodegang, the

Bishop-in-waiting of Metz and his entourage of priests and monks assembled before them on a raised section above the baptismal font.

The Bishop led the men in prayers for the salvation of the soul of the infant Waldo. He finished with a plea to God that Waldo's religious destiny would be fulfilled.

"As the second son, it will be Waldo's duty to save the family's souls for entry into the Kingdom of Heaven by devoting his life to the service of the Lord our God as a member of the clergy in the Holy Christian Church. Let us bow our heads in silent, fervent prayer that this is the will of the Lord and shall come to pass."

The Bishop blessed the assembled men and signaled for the main door to be opened once again.

High overhead the sun shone directly down on the church with a benevolent warmth. When the doors were opened a burst of golden light filled the baptistery, glistening brightly on the water in the baptismal font.

For the men already inside, the figures entering the church were silhouettes carried forward in a giant halo of sunshine. As they moved into the church out of the glare of the light behind them, their form and features came into clear focus.

Leading the group, carrying the infant Waldo, was a girl called Bertrada of Laon, a relation of Waldo's mother, Farahild, who as tradition decreed, was not present at her child's christening. Bertrada was accompanied by Waldo's godfather Pippin and his godmother the Duchess of Williswinda.

The Bishop of Metz was waiting just inside the entrance hall, ready to accept the child for baptism.

Bertrada presented the infant Waldo to the bishop, who was beaming with the joy of baptising his own nephew. But there were rituals to be followed as if he were anyone's newborn.

"Has the child been baptised before?" he asked.

"No your Grace." said Bertrada softly.

"Is the child a boy or a girl?" the bishop asked.

"He is a boy," Bertrada replied shyly, "his name shall be Waldo."

The bishop then blessed the infant Waldo and placed a pinch of salt in the child's mouth to represent the reception of wisdom and to exorcise any demons.

He then turned to the godparents.

"Do you both know the prayers you are to teach the child?"

"We do, your Grace," answered Pippin and the Duchess in unison.

With that, the bishop led the group to the baptismal font where he anointed the infant, immersed him in the font and named him Waldo.

His godfather, Pippin, raised him out of the water

and held him while his godmother wrapped him in a chryson, a christening gown of fine white linen decorated with glittering seed pearls.

†

The final part of the ceremony was to take place at the altar. Bertrada took Waldo from his godparents and going ahead of the others, carried him up to the altar, where she waited for the others to join her.

At this point it seemed that the sun moved suddenly in the sky as a shaft of light beamed in from a window high up in the nave and shone directly on Bertrada and the infant Waldo nestled in her arms.

A murmur rose from many among the gathering. Is it a sign from heaven? The God-light illuminating Waldo's certain destiny as a great holy man of the church. They saw the beam of golden light as a flame of devotion to the Lord and bowed their heads in silent adoration.

The only head not bowed was Pippin's, whose eyes were glowing with the flame of an entirely different kind of adoration. His gaze was fixed on the young Bertrada, as it had been throughout the baptism ceremony. Pippin saw the beam of light striking the beautiful countenance of Bertrada as a sign from God too, or at least from His cherubs, whose golden arrows had found their mark.

3

Love

"Love is the key that opens the gates of happiness," Duchess Williswinda said.

Pippin seemed not to hear. He was now standing right beside Bertrada at the altar, about to recite his godfather vows. The scent of her was intoxicating and making him feel light-headed. He was also having trouble breathing, and his pulse was racing.

Williswinda, Waldo's godmother, was standing at his other side.

"To love is to receive a glimpse of heaven," she said softly, close to Pippin's ear.

His face flushed a deep scarlet, but he refused to look at the Duchess, who was smiling broadly. She seemed to have read his most intimate thoughts. Pippin was indeed thinking that the golden sunlight illuminating Bertrada's dazzling garment of white silk and bleached linen, transformed her into an angel sent from heaven.

He felt a gentle nudge in his ribs from Williswinda, who was enjoying herself immensely at Pippin's expense.

He realised that the Bishop was looking directly at him with a patient smile on his face.

"Forgive me, your Grace," Pippin said, recovering

quickly, as a great leader should. "I was lost in thoughts of the divine beauty of this holy ceremony."

Waldo's godmother snorted as she stifled a laugh, attracting a knowing look from the bishop, who was fighting his own battle trying not to laugh on such a devout occasion.

Once the baptism ritual had finished, Pippin found the courage to turn and look directly at Bertrada, who rewarded him with a glorious smile that lit up his soul and shone out through his eyes.

He was oblivious to the many other smiles on the faces around him who recognized a man hopelessly smitten by love.

To bring Pippin back to reality and the matters at hand, Richbold stepped forward.

"Our great and revered Lords, Pippin and Karlman," he announced loudly, "My beloved wife Farahild and I are honoured, on behalf of the Duchess Williswinda, to invite you, and all our friends gathered here, to join us across the river Rhine at Lorsch, the Duchess's family estate.

The holy baptism of my son Waldo has taken place in the sight of God and his heavenly angels. Now we celebrate this blissful event with the joy of earthly pleasures - beer, wine, food, dancing and singing - in the company of my beloved wife Farahild, who, as per tradition was not present during this holy ceremony!"

The ripeness of summer filled the afternoon air with gentle warmth and rich fragrances of the lush countryside as the happy gathering left the church.

While they made their way across the Rhine, preparations for the celebration feast were almost complete. A large striped tent, festooned with colourful flags and banners fluttering in the gentle breeze, stood in a wide, grassy clearing near a grove of fruit trees. Some distance away under a stand of spruce trees, a cluster of smaller tents waited to welcome the exhausted revellers at the end of the day.

Inside the main tent, a long wide table of polished oak overflowed with delicious food of every kind – roasted meats and fish, fruit and vegetables, freshly baked breads, jugs of wine and small barrels of dark beer made from barley, mead and wine.

The Duchess's young son Cancor had arranged the feast and he was still buzzing to and fro attending to last minute details as the guests began arriving. From the moment the first beers were handed around to eager hands, the festivities were in full swing. The tantalising aroma of pork and lamb roasting on spits over open fires was irresistible. The hearty feasting began without delay, and continued throughout the afternoon, amplified with much mirth and merriment.

By the time the sun began to melt into the horizon, the abundance of food, drink and sunshine had taken its toll. In the lingering pink afterglow of sunset, shadowy figures, on unsteady feet, began to drift off to their tents under the spruce trees. The long day of exuberant celebration and overindulgence had exhausted almost everyone.

One man, though, had reserved his energy. Throughout the festivities, Pippin had been restrained in the drinking activities. For most of the day his mind had been preoccupied with finding a way to spend time alone with Bertrada that evening, in secret. Yet, after all that thinking, he had come up with no plan. Even taking the initiative and approaching her directly seemed beyond him.

As he sat by the glowing embers of one of the spit roasting fires pondering his dilemma, he saw Bertrada at the entrance of the main tent in conversation with Duchess Williswinda. As he watched them, both turned and looked in his direction.

"I think we should go and say goodnight to our lord Pippin." the Duchess said. "Are you happy to do that, my dear?"

Bertrada smiled sweetly and nodded.

As they approached Pippin, he stood up and greeted them.

"My ladies," he said, with a subtle dip of his head.

"My lord," Duchess Williswinda replied. "It has been a wonderful day. And baby Waldo is greatly privileged to have you as his godfather."

"And truly honoured to have such a godmother as you, my lady," Pippin said.

"I must bid you good night, my lord," Williswinda said. "We have another full day tomorrow." She smiled at him. "Can I leave the lovely Bertrada in your capable hands? Will you see her safely to her tent?"

"Of course, my lady," Pippin replied, embracing her gently.

Williswinda embraced Bertrada, smiled again at Pippin, and then left, leaving the two of them standing either side of the fire staring into each other's eyes. The soft light from the fire's embers added a pink blush to Bertrada's face and a glow in her eyes.

At the touch of love, Plato said, everyone becomes a poet. That night, by the fire, the poet buried deep inside Pippin miraculously emerged for a few fleeting seconds from some hidden recess of his heart and uttered a declaration of love.

"If the only place where I could see you was in my dreams," he said softly, "I'd like to sleep forever."

Bertrada bowed her head.

"My Lord," she said, "a dream is a wish the heart makes."

The warm night air wrapped around them like an

embrace. They strolled through the grove of fruit trees behind the main tent for several hours talking about nothing, and everything. Bertrada's innocence and Pippin's shyness in love heightened the wonder of a tender passion neither had known before.

Sometime before dawn they found themselves lying together on sheepskin rugs in the main tent. They had both enjoyed some of the wine still in a jug on the banquet table.

In a blissful hour before the birdsong heralded the new day, Pippin and Bertrada created a new life destined to change the course of history. They made a son who would become the greatest Emperor King of the European Middle Ages - Charlemagne - Charles the Great.

4

Death

The morning sun was high above the horizon before the first of the previous day's revellers emerged bleary-eyed from their tents to face the glare of the bright summer sky.

A few, however, were not so sluggish. Cancor and his staff had risen early and cleared the table in the main tent of the remains of the previous day's feast and re-laid it with fresh food and drinks for breakfast. It included many barrels of spring water that would be in great demand when the guests first entered the tent. By midday most of them were up and about and slowly recovering their enthusiasm for another afternoon of feasting and festivities.

Pippin and Bertrada had left the tent before the clean-up began just after first light, and almost no-one was aware of their illicit love tryst in the bewitching hours before dawn. Only the Duchess Williswinda, who was partly complicit in the liaison, knew when she saw Bertrada's radiant expression that the passion of love had claimed her heart. But even the Duchess had no way of knowing that an extraordinary new life had sprung forth in the heat of that passion.

For Pippin, however, there was no time to bask in the glow of new found love. As he watched Bertrada taking the baby Waldo from his mother Farahild's arms and placing him in a cradle in the shade of a canopy, a messenger arrived with grave news: Pippin and Karlman's father, Charles Martel, the Hammer, lies dying at Quierzy-sur-Oise and has called for his two sons to go to him.

Before dawn the next day, the two brothers and their retinue set off from Worms on the week-long journey west to Quierzy.

†

The mood on the journey was solemn, but not morose. Both men knew this time would come eventually. The prospect of their father's death was something they had learnt to live with from the time they were young boys. They grew up expecting any day to hear that he had been killed in battle.

That he survived so many brutal and bloody encounters was a continuous miracle that only God could claim credit for. They were taught that even the greatest warriors, like their father, usually died on the battlefield, and they had accepted that was the way it would be. So it was always a surprise, and a joy, whenever he returned safely.

"What will you say to him?" Karlman asked his brother.

"I will tell him that he is the hero of the age," Pippin said. "That his many victories have improved the happiness of mankind for centuries to come. And you, Karlman?"

"You know, my brother," Karlman said, "our father never cared for prestige and titles so long as the real power was in his hands. He never called himself King. But I will tell him he is the greatest King there ever was, or will be."

"Yes!" Pippin declared. "We will tell him that he deserves to become the father of a long line of great kings."

"Starting with us," Karlman said. "That is our duty, and homage, to him."

For some time, the brothers rode without speaking, lost in their own thoughts, before Karlman broke the silence.

"I trust we are not too late," he said quietly.

"Fear not, brother!" Pippin responded brightly. "Our father is a brilliant tactician ... he would not leave it too late to call us. He would not fail in his final duty to tell us what we need to hear."

Pippin knew his father well. Charles Martel had allowed himself plenty of time to farewell his sons and pass on his wishes and demands of them as his successors. The three men spent many weeks together reliving the patriarch's decades of great military successes and political victories.

The invincible arm of the Hammer, Charles Martel, saved and delivered Europe and Christianity from the deadly grasp of the all-conquering power of Islam. He had halted the Muslim Moors on their destructive path of continental domination. And he changed most of Europe from a horde of barbarian rabble constantly fighting with one another, to a civilized and organized state.

The Hammer's boots had marched triumphantly against Muslim, Saxon and many other invaders time and time again in his ferocious defence of Western Europe and Christendom.

For his sons, they were massive, intimidating boots to fill, perhaps several sizes too massive. Nonetheless, they had to fill them very soon.

Pippin and Karlman were acutely aware of the formidable military leader their father had been and the extraordinary legacy he left them.

They knew it would take the two of them to replace the single towering figure of the Hammer. Just as they knew there would be no time to mourn their father as there were many battles waiting to be fought throughout their lands.

Charles Martel died on September 28th, 741 at Quierzy-sur-Oise leaving his two sons to take up where he left off. Together, Pippin and Karlman were up to the task and continued to defend European Christendom and build the Carolingian empire. Their father's territories were divided between them. Karlman took over as ruler of Austrasia, Alemannia and Bavaria. Pippin became ruler of Neustria, Burgundy and Aquitaine.

Neither brother disputed their father's decision. They were content with their spoils and didn't see one another as competitors. The only disgruntled member of the family was their new brother-in-law, the Bavarian Duke Odillo, who had recently married their sister Hiltrude.

"Odillo thinks we are pretenders and he is the legitimate ruler of Europe," Karlman said.

"Just like any noble," Pippin replied, "Odillo thinks birthright is superior to power and might. We will correct his error one way or another."

"He is already rallying the Swabian mobs to his cause."

"Well, brother," Pippin said, "Against the two of us, they have no chance."

"I trust our sister will understand," Karlman said.

"Let's just hope her new husband isn't killed in the battle," Pippin said. "Hiltrude would never forgive us."

Hiltrude's forgiveness was never tested. Pippin and Karlman met Duke Odillo's forces on the battlefield in the Alsace and won a convincing victory over their rebellious brother-in-law.

The Duke survived the battle and continued to rule Bavaria as a feudal lord under Karlman's authority.

5

Refuge

In Pippin's mind, his hurried departure from the christening celebrations at Worms had virtually wrenched him physically from Bertrada's arms. There had been no opportunity to say goodbye properly, as new, passionate lovers should.

Even if he wasn't prepared to admit it to himself, it had been a wrenching of his heart as well. Many times during the two months in Quierzy before his father died, he had been thinking of Bertrada and longing for her embrace. He wasn't to know that he had seeded a bud of life in Bertrada's womb, which was blossoming vigorously with each day that passed.

Bertrada was longing for Pippin too, and to share the news that she was pregnant with his child. No-one else could know Pippin was the father, so she had to keep their secret to herself. She felt it was Pippin's decision to reveal the truth, or not. In the meantime though, Bertrada was simply pregnant and unmarried, and her fate was sealed.

Her family abandoned her and would have nothing more to do with her. She was cast out without mercy and faced a bleak future as a young mother with no husband to support and protect her.

At this time Richbold was ordered by Pippin and Karlman to move his family from near Worms, and take them south, to a town near Strassburg on the river Rhine.

"Bertrada, we are moving to Burkheim," Waldo's mother, Farahild, said. "We are to administer the Breisgau, and the most important Rhine crossing in the region, on behalf of Pippin and Karlman. You are welcome to come and live with us there, where you and your baby will be safe, and you will be part of our family. We are related after all."

Bertrada was overcome with joy and gratitude and wept openly, unable to speak. Farahild hugged her tightly.

"We are to live in a restored Roman castello," she said, brightly. "It has under floor heating, all the amenities we need ... and we can bathe in warm water all year round!"

Through her tears, Bertrada managed a smile.

"I will never forget your love and kindness, Farahild," she said.

And neither will my child ... and its father, she thought, if he does not, God forbid, forsake me.

†

For several months Bertrada lived happily with Waldo's family and tenderly nurtured the life growing inside her. Deep in her heart though, she was anxious about how Pippin would react when he found out the child was his. Would he accept it, and her, or reject them both? And how was she to get the news to him? It was her secret until she could tell him herself.

Having settled into their new home and their duties managing the Breisgau crossing, Richbold's household was looking ahead to Christmas and making plans for the holy devotions and festive celebrations.

After dinner one evening with friends and important guests from Burkheim, Richbold rose from his chair to make an announcement.

"My friends, Christmas is only weeks away, and we are all busy preparing for this wonderful and holy time of prayer and celebration. Along with all our family and friends, this year we will be honoured by the presence of two exalted guests."

Bertrada gasped involuntarily, and then instantly stifled it, pretending to cough.

Richbold exchanged a brief knowing smile with his wife, unseen by Bertrada.

"Pippin and Karlman will be joining us!" he said.

†

"Let me feel our child," Pippin said tenderly, the moment he saw Bertrada.

As he gently ran his hand over her swollen belly, he felt a sharp kick.

"I'm sure it's a boy, he has a strong kick," he declared, laughing.

Bertrada had said nothing, she was simply staring at him in astonishment.

"But, how did you know?" she finally managed to say.

"My darling," he said, embracing her carefully. "Farahild and the Duchess Williswinda are most perceptive and resourceful ladies. They found a way to advise me of their suspicions. I am overjoyed. The spirit of my father lives on! Here in your belly. He will be called Charles, after him. Our son - grandson of the mighty Hammer!"

Pippin's joy at the prospect of a son and heir was tempered by the certainty that when the worst of winter was over, he would be required on the battlefields once again. With Charles Martel dead, many of the Hammer's enemies who did not dare fight him, now saw an opportunity to strike before his two sons could firmly establish their power as his successors.

The Alemanni, Bavarians and Saxons were all out for

revenge, and the Muslim Moors were planning new invasions across the Pyrenees into southern Europe.

Pippin spent as much time as he could with Bertrada after Christmas, but by March the demands of war had overtaken him. Less than a month before his first son was born, he went off to the battlefields leaving a distraught Bertrada to bring their son into the world without him by her side.

6

Childhood

Only the soft glow of candles illuminated Bertrada's exhausted face as she lay recovering in the warm darkness of the birthing room. For one so young, she had faced the terror of her first childbirth with extraordinary courage and dignity. She had heard that labour pain could be unbearable, and that it was women's punishment for Eve's eternal sin.

But God had been kind and merciful to her with her first birth. Her son Charles had seemed in a great hurry to come into the world and Bertrada's ordeal was over quickly. She could hear him protesting loudly in the next room as the midwife wrapped him in swaddling clothes to protect him from the influence of evil spirits until baptism. Bertrada sighed with happiness and Charles's cries faded as she drifted into a deep sleep.

†

"Behold the newest addition to our family," Richbold announced to the gathered household, holding the swaddled infant in his arms. "Charles, son of Pippin and Bertrada, and grandson of Charles Martel. Born strong and healthy, by the grace of God, on this glorious day April 2nd, 742."

"What do you think, Waldo?" Farahild said, holding her son close to the infant Charles so that their noses were almost touching.

Waldo was still an infant himself, only about one year old. He smiled and gurgled happily. He reached out and put his hand on Charles's forehead, who was wrapped tightly like a tiny mummy in his swaddling clothes and could only mimic Waldo's smile and gurgle.

"Ah, look!" Farahild said. "They are best friends already." She kissed Waldo and held him up in front of her face. "Good boy my darling Waldo," she said. "You must always look after Charles, like an older brother."

†

Whether it was just her youth, or if her distress at Pippin's absence also contributed to it, Bertrada was unable to lactate and could not suckle her infant son. Farahild was still breastfeeding baby Waldo and offered to provide milk for the infant Charles as well.

However, she quickly became ill and was growing weaker by the day. Finally, Farahild was unable to breastfeed either Waldo or Charles and a milk mother, called Anneliese, was employed to take her place. Sadly, not long after, Farahild died of exhaustion.

Waldo was still too young for the tragic loss of his mother to affect him, but it was a devastating blow to his older brother Ruthard who took many years to come to terms with it. The personalities of the two brothers were very different from that point on.

Both Waldo and Charles grew to love their milk mother Anneliese, a Swabian girl from Birkenfeld. She had a gift for storytelling and would keep the boys entranced for hours with her wonderful fables and tales of pagan legends and Christian religion.

One day Anneliese told Waldo and Charles the story of two famous martyrs, Nazarius and Celsus. Perhaps at some point later on Anneliese wished she had not told the boys the martyrs' story because they could not get enough of it and wanted to hear it over and over again. But Anneliese loved the boys as they loved her, and she never tired of telling them about Nazarius and Celsus.

"It was the time of the Roman Emperor Nero," Anneliese began.

Waldo and Charles had heard this opening sentence so many times they could recite it in their sleep, but each time Anneliese spoke the words it sent the boys into a trance of attention. They sat perfectly still, wide-eyed and open-mouthed.

"Nero was persecuting the Christians," Anneliese continued, "and it was a dangerous place for Nazarius, who lived in Rome with his parents. His mother was the Christian Perpetua and his father was the Jew Africanus. Nazarius, adopting his mother's religion, wanted to preach about Jesus and help wandering Christians, so he fled from Rome and preached in Lombardy. There he went to Milan where he met the twin brothers Gervase and Protase. The brothers had been born into a rich Roman family. But they were left orphans because their parents Vitalius and Valeria were martyred for their Christian faith. Gervase and Protase gave their wealth to the poor, set their slaves free and spent their time fasting and praying. Nero's pagan soldiers locked them up in prison for their confession of faith in Jesus."

Anneliese deliberately paused before continuing to add some tension to her storytelling.

"Nazarius wanted to help the twin brothers," she said, "and he tried to relieve their sufferings. But you know what happened then?"

The boys just stared at her, waiting.

"The horrible pagans punished him!" she declared dramatically. "They gave him a terrible beating and banished him from Milan! Just for trying to help ease the pain of his Christian friends."

"Those pagans and Nero were evil," Waldo said to Charles, who nodded vigorously.

"When he recovered from his beating," Anneliese said, "Nazarius went to Embrun where he was allowed to preach about Jesus. He was very good at explaining the holiness and love of Jesus and convinced many heathens to become Christians. And he did it gently just by telling stories of good Christians like Gervase and Protase. He didn't have to threaten them with the fires of hell because they trusted him and believed he was telling the truth."

At this point Waldo was smiling broadly as always because he liked the idea that the pagans weren't forced to convert through fear of God's wrath, or the brutality of the sword. Being a little younger than Waldo, perhaps Charles wasn't able to understand the significance of gentle persuasion and he didn't return Waldo's smile when he looked at him. Instead he pleaded with Anneliese.

"Tell us about Celsus!" he cried.

"Well," Anneliese said, "in the city of Kimel, Nazarius baptised the young son of a certain Christian widow. The boy's name was Celsus, and he became a faithful student of Nazarius and helped him in his missionary work."

Now Waldo and Charles were getting excited and couldn't wait for Anneliese to tell them the next part of the story.

"The pagans hated Nazarius and Celsus for preaching

about Jesus, and so they decided they should be devoured by wild beasts."

Anneliese knew what was coming next and pretended to be distracted by something and again paused in her story. Waldo and Charles were beside themselves with anticipation, calling to her to continue. After several more seconds teasing the boys, she went on.

"Now where was I?" she said. "Oh yes, I remember ... when Nazarius and Celsus were thrown in the cage with the wild beasts, they refused to eat them!"

Waldo and Charles went wild, clapping and cheering wildly, jumping up and down on the spot.

Anneliese waited for them to calm down and continued.

"Then afterwards, the pagan soldiers were ordered to drown them into the river Mosel, near Trier, by throwing them overboard. But a storm was brewing just when they reached the middle of the wide river, putting enormous fear into the soldiers. Nazarius calmed their souls with a prayer to God the Almighty and promised their safe return if he and Celsus were released. So it was done and all were saved and the Christians released."

There were more noisy celebrations from Waldo and Charles. But it was briefer and more subdued because they knew how the story ended.

"After this miraculous encounter, Nazarius and

Celsus felt invincible. They returned to Milan and visited Gervase and Protase in prison. Unfortunately this was a big mistake and they were arrested and taken to Nero. This pagan emperor ordered that Nazarius and Celsus be beheaded."

Waldo and Charles sat silently staring at Anneliese with tears welling up in their eyes.

"Many years later," Anneliese said, "during the reign of the holy Emperor Theodosius, Saint Ambrose, the Bishop of Milan, made an amazing discovery after being given a sign by God. In a garden outside the city walls he found the remains of Nazarius, including his severed head. Nazarius's blood was reportedly still liquid and red when his body was taken by Saint Ambrose to the Basilica of the Apostles. In the same garden he also discovered the remains of Saint Celsus, which he also had taken to the Basilica."

"But Nazarius and Celsus are now Saints in heaven with God," Waldo said, wiping his eyes with one hand and putting his other arm around Charles, who still had tears streaming down his cheeks.

†

When it was time for the boys to be confirmed as Christians, there was no difficulty for Richbold in choosing each one's confirmation name, which tradition demanded must be the name of a saint. Waldo and Charles were confirmed as Nazarius and Celsus.

Like their favourite martyrs, the two boys were inseparable and devoted to one another. It was a bond forged in childhood that would never be broken as both followed their different destinies to become great men of the time.

However, fulfilling those destinies was many years in the future. For now, in the beautiful countryside of the Upper Rhineland at the Breisgau crossing, Waldo and Charles enjoyed a lifestyle every young boy dreams of. They lived in a fortress by the river, surrounded by meadows, vineyards, dark forests, and they enjoyed all the privileges of being part of a noble family who wanted for nothing.

7

Schooling

As was the tradition, in the summer months Richbold invited a learned monk to live in the castello on the Breisgau to further the education of his sons Ruthard and Waldo, and also the young Charles, who was approaching the learning age.

"Well, boys, I have some exciting news for you," Richbold said to his two sons and Charles one Sunday morning while they were all out in the courtyard enjoying the sunshine.

"A very holy and educated monk called Othmar is coming to live with us for a while to teach you many interesting and wonderful things. You will learn about Latin, the arts, numbers and even Gregorian chanting. He will also show you how to grow herbs and teach you about their marvellous healing powers."

Charles was still a little too young to fully understand, but Waldo looked wide-eyed and excited at the news about the monk Othmar. Ruthard, on the other hand, seemed less than enthusiastic.

Richbold had anticipated Ruthard's negative reaction.

"And Ruthard, I have also invited Warin to join us, so you will have your best friend here with you and you can learn from Othmar together."

Despite Ruthard's lack of enthusiasm, the boys were fortunate indeed to have Othmar as their tutor. He had been greatly admired and respected as a monk and teacher by Charles Martel, the Hammer, Charles's grandfather.

Over several summers of tuition by Othmar, Waldo and Charles proved to be bright and eager students who wanted to learn everything Othmar had to teach them, with the exception, perhaps, of Latin. They particularly loved growing herbs, and of course, they couldn't get enough of all the martyr stories Othmar knew so well. Waldo also discovered that he possessed an extraordinary memory for details, especially when it came to remembering herbs, the medicinal ones and the poisonous ones.

The two younger boys' eagerness to learn wasn't shared by Ruthard and Warin, who were far more interested in playing at sword fighting and hearing about great warriors and their exciting deeds on the battlefields.

Othmar refused to teach them such things and constantly berated the two older boys for their disobedience and bad behaviour.

Luckily for Ruthard and Warin, however, there were breaks from the hated Latin and herb growing lessons and they had some adventures to enjoy. The boys were allowed to observe a hunt in the Black Forrest, and Richbold took them on a trip to the Alsace, where they took a small boat to a nearby island in the Rhine river.

Waldo proved to be a keen sailor.

"Look Charles," he cried, "if you lean over you can put your hand in the water! Come on, try it."

"Be careful, Waldo, don't lean too far over," Richbold warned.

"Lean as far as you can, Waldo!" Ruthard called out, provoking loud laughter from Warin.

No amount of coaxing from Waldo was going to convince Charles to lean over and feel the water. He seemed terrified of falling overboard and stayed away from the sides of the boat.

"It's too wobbly," he said. "We will tip over."

At that, Ruthard and Warin started to deliberately rock the boat, producing screams of terror from Charles, until Richbold quickly called a halt to their mischief.

The trip also gave the four boys the chance to visit the old Roman settlement of Augusta Raurica and the village of Saint-Hippolyte, where they stayed over night with a Christian friend called Fulrad.

The next day, Ruthard and Warin were even allowed

to ride horses. It was an exciting time for all the boys, but it was over too soon. Before long they were back at Burkheim, resuming their lessons with Othmar. Waldo and Charles were happy to see him, but Ruthard and Warin became more sullen and disobedient than ever.

One day they decided to take their frustrations out on Charles. Some days it was Waldo they picked on, but this time Charles was the victim of their malevolence. At the end of the day's lessons after Othmar had left them, Warin started to waddle around the room and make noises like a duck. Waldo and Charles thought it was funny at first, until Warin said, "Ruthard, who do you think I am when I walk like this?" He then proceeded to totter around with an even more pronounced waddle.

Ruthard stood watching with his arms folded staring at the ceiling with an exaggerated look of perplexity.

"Well, let me think who it could be .... um, is it .... Bertrada?" he said with a childish smile.

At that, both he and Warin burst into laughter. Charles's reaction was instant, and he moved so fast that Warin was taken by surprise. Charles flew at his tormenter in a rage, grabbing him by the hair with one hand and digging the fingers of the other into his face. He inflicted several deep scratches on Warin's cheek before Waldo and Ruthard could drag him off.

Warin was incensed and about to attack Charles when

Richbold arrived to see what all the commotion was about. The two older boys tried to explain it away as just high-spirited play, but Richbold could see that Charles was deeply upset.

"We'll discuss this later, Ruthard," he said tersely as he led Charles away.

"I'm going to beat that little fiend to a pulp," Warin said when he rubbed his cheek and realised that Charles had drawn blood.

"You lay a finger on Charles," Waldo said, "and I'll tell Bertrada what you said about her."

Warin glowered at Waldo but said nothing as he dabbed at his wounded cheek with a piece of cloth.

"What was all that about, Ruthard," Waldo said. "Why was Charles so upset?"

"We didn't think he'd go crazy ... like a wild animal," Ruthard said. "We've teased him many times before. We all know he's got a temper, but he's never been crazy like that."

"What was the duck waddle all about?" Waldo asked.

Ruthard shrugged. "I thought you knew – Charles obviously does. Bertrada has large feet that point outwards a little when she walks, so she waddles. She's known around as 'goose-foot.'"

"I couldn't do a goose noise," Warin said, still scowling and dabbing at his cheek.

During the summer months, the two older boys learnt nothing from Othmar. All they gained was a hatred for their tutor that would continue into their adult lives, and one day result in Othmar's tragic exile and death.

8

Reunited

"My father is coming to see us!" Charles exclaimed. "I will finally meet him. Mother says he might take us on an adventure with him!"

Charles, now eight years old, never met his father, Pippin and was highly excited when Ruthard told him of his imminent arrival.

Waldo was excited too, and happy for Charles, as he knew, how hurt he was by not knowing his father.

"Where will he take us?" Waldo said, wide-eyed.

"I'll ask mother," Charles called over his shoulder as he ran off to find Bertrada.

Bertrada wasn't easy to find. She had locked herself in a dark room, lit only by a single large candle, and was on her knees praying to a golden statue of the Virgin Mary. She could hear Charles calling for her but ignored him and went on praying.

"Blessed Mother of God," she whispered, "please instil in Pippin the desire for marriage, and if we are worthy, grant us the joy of another child."

Outside the room, Charles had finally tracked her down

and was banging on the door.

With a sigh, Bertrada rose to her feet, blew out the candle and opened the door. In her son's large, excited eyes, she saw his father's strength and determination. She also saw the face of an illegitimate son. As she hugged him to her and kissed him on the cheek, she prayed silently that he would soon be Pippin's legitimate son, and she a married mother.

†

From the tower of Richbold's fortress, Waldo and Charles began watching Pippin and his men approaching when they were still a long way off. They were at least an hour away and just specks in the distance, but the two boys didn't take their eyes off them until they rode in the front gates. Waldo and Charles raced down the tower steps with reckless abandon, oblivious to the cries of concern from both Richbold and Bertrada.

"Waldo! Charles!" Richbold yelled. "Slow down or you'll break your necks!"

His pleas went unheeded. The boys burst through the front door at a run and down the wide steps to the gatehouse courtyard. The sound of ten horses hooves on the cobblestones was loud enough to make conversation difficult, but Charles's excited voice cut through clearly.

"Father! Father!" he yelled. "You're here! You're here!"

Pippin dismounted in one smooth movement, just in time to sweep Charles up off the ground, who had virtually leapt into his arms.

"Yes – I'm here, son!" he said, hugging Charles and kissing him on the forehead.

Bertrada appeared at the top of the steps in the front entrance.

"Ah, there's your beautiful mother," Pippin said, smiling broadly. "Let's go to her – I have some wonderful news for Bertrada. And for you and Waldo, too!"

"Are you taking us on an adventure?!" Charles cried.

"I'm going to take you both with me to the foot of the Alps, to meet the Pope."

The boys' screeches of delight echoed around the courtyard, startling the horses.

†

Whether Richbold thought it a good idea that his young son travel to the Alps without his father, he didn't say. Pippin had decreed it to be so, deciding that Charles needed his best friend Waldo to be on the journey with him. And by then, to object would have achieved nothing but devastating disappointment for Waldo.

As it turned out, Pippin didn't actually take the boys

to Switzerland but sent them on ahead. Waldo, Charles, Ruthard and Warin, together with an entourage of dignitaries, such as the Alsacian family friend Fulrad, by now the Bishop of St. Denis' Abbey, met the Pope before Pippin arrived.

The boys weren't particularly impressed and decided afterwards that the Holy Father was a bit of a grumpy old man. Understandably, Pope Stephen II wasn't at all happy that instead of being met by the king, he was greeted by his young son and some other young boys.

All was forgiven however, when Pippin's army decimated the Lombard forces and restored the Pope's power in Rome. Pippin's victory on the Pope's behalf resulted in him becoming the first Carolingian King anointed by the Pope at a lavish ceremony at the Basilica of St. Denis in Paris in 754. His coronation and that of his sons on the same day began the Carolingian royal dynasty.

The grateful Pope also helped answer Bertrada's prayers. He had no hesitation in allowing her and Pippin to marry at last, despite the fact that they were closely related as cousins.

The wedding took place at the Prüm Abbey, which was founded by Bertrada's grandmother in 720AD. This ceremony not only made Bertrada the Queen of the Franks, but it also reunited her with her family, who welcomed her home with open arms.

A divine wedding present came from the Pope, Stephen II. He sent one of Christendom's most incredible relics, the sandals of Jesus Christ the Saviour.

The Lord God also intervened and granted her wish for another child. In early spring the following year, Carloman was born as a legitimate heir to Pippin's crown.

9

Ravenna

For Charles, the illegitimate heir to the Carolingian royal dynasty, life was one exciting adventure after another. And living with his best friend Waldo made it all that much better.

A year after they met the Pope, Charles and Waldo were travelling across the Alps into northern Italy with Pippin's army, to the cities of Ravenna and Pavia.

Waldo and Charles were still young teenagers, embarking on their greatest adventure together, before their destinies took them in vastly different directions. It was their first trip to Ravenna, an important city in history as the capital of the Western Roman Empire in the 5th century, and Byzantine Italy in the centuries following.

Soon after they reached Ravenna, Pippin's forces drove the Lombards out of the city. Several years later, in 756, he gifted Ravenna to the Pope.

After the Lombards had left, chased by Pippin's soldiers, Waldo and Charles were shown around the city. Everywhere they looked they saw new things that fascinated them, especially the buildings. What excited them the most was the magnificent octagon church of San Vitale. They could immediately see why their teacher Othmar had spoken of it with such awe. Just as he had told them it would, its inspiring beauty took their breath away.

"It is as if the heavens and the earth were touching," Othmar had said. "You feel that the Almighty God Himself is there with you and your prayers will be answered immediately."

The boys felt privileged to enter the presbytery, which is a part of the church for the use of the clergy only. Waldo was completely mesmerized by the stunning vaulted ceiling soaring high above them. He felt at home, as if he belonged there.

He gazed up in wonder at the richly ornamented mosaic walls and ceilings covered with a mass of colourful leaves, fruit, flowers, stars, animals and birds, including many peacocks. At the very centre was a crown encircling the Lamb of God, supported by four angels.

In the middle hung an octagon chandelier engraved with a message for the pilgrims, which read: ‚Sic currite ut comprehendatis' which means one must ‘Walk in order to understand'. There were also the words: ‘Claudius audeat vincere' - ‘Claudius would risk it to win'.

Charles was more interested in the power and wealth the great church represented.

"Father tells me this church cost 26,000 solidi to build ... 26,000 solid gold coins! Can you believe it? Imagine how powerful you would be with that much money to spend on a church."

"It's over 200 years old," Waldo said, still staring upwards. "And it took almost 20 years to build. It was started by a bishop in 527 and completed by another bishop in 546."

"You'll have to build something even better when you're a bishop, Waldo."

Waldo dragged his eyes down from the ceiling and frowned at Charles.

He rubbed his neck vigorously, which was aching from prolonged staring at the ceiling.

"Who says I'm going to be a bishop?"

"I do," Charles said. "When I'm king, I'll make you a bishop. The most important bishop in the world."

"I might not want to be a bishop," Waldo argued.

"You have to be," Charles replied. "You can't be king, because I will be. But you can be the next best thing – the Imperial Bishop of all Christendom!"

Charles had yelled out the word 'Christendom' at the top of his voice and it echoed throughout the church.

†

The boys continued their wide-eyed exploration of San Vitale.

"Look, Charles," Waldo said, "here's a plaque with a plan of the church."

"It's got eight sides," Charles said.
"An octagon," Waldo explained.

"I know that," Charles replied sharply. "Why is it an octagon?"

"Eight is a special symbolic number in Christianity," Waldo said. "Remember? ... Othmar taught us that. Christ rose from the dead eight days after he was arrested in Jerusalem - before he was crucified. His resurrection awakened the hope for a new creation and the end of fear and darkness. And also, the world began on the eighth day after the seven days of creation. So the number eight symbolises rebirth and renewal. That's why most baptismal fonts are octagonal."

Charles was applauding loudly.

"See, Waldo! That's why you'll be a bishop. You already talk like one!"

"I can also talk like an architect," Waldo said. "So maybe I'll be one of those instead."

"What do you mean?" Charles said.

"I know about the Sacred Cut."

"The what?"

"The Sacred Cut – it's an easy way to accurately draw an octagon," Waldo explained. "You simply draw a square. Then place a compass at each corner and draw an arc that passes through the centre of the square and intersects two sides of the square. Do that four times. When you connect the eight points where the compass lines intersect the sides, cut off the four corners of the square, then you have an octagon."

"We'll try it when we get home," Charles said, trying not to look too impressed with Waldo's knowledge. Just then, something caught his eye and he hurried off to the far end of the presbytery.

"There's also an octagonal baptistery here in Ravenna that was built over 300 years ago," Waldo called after him. "Let's go and see that."

"Look here, Waldo!" Charles yelled a minute later. "Come over here!"

Waldo found Charles studying a large, colourful mosaic panel depicting the East Roman Emperor Justinian I, clad in purple with a golden halo, standing next to court officials, including a bishop, soldiers and priests. The Emperor was in the middle, with soldiers on his right and clergy on his left.

"This is symbolism I know about," Charles said, tapping his finger on the figure of the emperor. "It says that the emperor is the leader of both church and state of his empire."

Waldo nodded in agreement. "You're right."

"That's how it will be with you and me, Waldo," Charles said. "There's me, the emperor in the centre. And there's the next most important person, you, the bishop, standing beside me. There are my soldiers, and there are your priests. We'll be an invincible team!"

Charles's large eyes were gleaming with excitement and Waldo marvelled at their brilliance and intensity. He found them almost mesmerising. At that moment he felt a strange sensation that he hadn't experienced before. As he stared at his friend's eyes, a clear vision filled his mind.

He saw a future Charles as a general leading his army across the countryside. A ball of fire traversed the sky and frightened his charger. Charles was thrown off the horse and lay on the ground without his weapons and cloak, the symbols of his authority. He had to be picked up by his servants who could see that the buckle of his cloak was broken and his baldric torn. Charles's spooked charger was nowhere to be seen. Suddenly Charles was remounted complete with his cloak and weapons, except he was now riding an elephant.

Waldo heard Charles calling out his name and felt him shaking him by the shoulders. He was aware of Charles's concerned face inches from his own.

Charles relaxed his grip. "You were in some kind of trance, Waldo," he said.

"I had a vision of you – it might be an omen! I saw you as a general leading your soldiers, when a fireball appeared in the sky and frightened your horse, throwing you off."

"I hope the tail of the fireball didn't touch the earth," Charles said with a smile. "The Romans call them comets and they believe if the tail touches the earth it means the end of the world."

"When you were mounted again you were riding an elephant!"

"It's a shame I don't believe in omens," Charles said laughing, "because I've always wanted one of those legendary Persian war elephants. Perhaps I'll ask my father to get me one."

"Then my vision will come true and it will be an omen." Waldo exclaimed.

"No it won't, Waldo. It will just mean my father got me an elephant." Charles laughed out loud.

Waldo looked shaken, he hadn't experienced visions before. He didn't like the feeling at all and tried to put it out of his mind. Charles seemed to have already forgotten it and returned his attention to the mosaic of Emperor Justinian.

10

Agony

From Ravenna, Pippin and his victorious army journeyed northwest to Pavia, the capital of the Kingdom of the Lombards.

Waldo and Charles looked on as Pippin signed the Peace Treaty of Pavia with the vanquished Lombard King Aistulf. It was an unconditional surrender of the lands of the Christian Church to Pope Stephen.

Just like the Church of San Vitale, the pomp and ceremony of Pippin's grand entrance and occupation of Pavia was awe-inspiring for Charles and Waldo.

They had never seen such dazzling pageantry and fanfare. The glorious beauty of a church equalled by the splendid spectacle of an army.

Waldo was watching Charles's reaction as much as the ceremony itself. His friend was completely mesmerised, but he also seemed overwhelmed by the almost frightening magnificence of it all.

It occurred to Waldo that Charles was just beginning to understand the awesome destiny that lay ahead of him. At that moment he also understood that his own destiny may be awesome too and that he should start preparing himself for it in mind, body and spirit.

†

The first big test of Waldo's strength of mind and spirit was waiting for him when he returned to Burkheim from his adventure across the Alps. He arrived home to find that his beloved father was dead. Waldo, and his brother Ruthard, were consumed by grief. For Waldo, the sense of loss was perhaps even greater because he had not been present when Richbold died and his father was already buried when he got home.

He had not even been at his own father's funeral. He had not said goodbye to the person he loved most on earth. Waldo and Ruthard felt that their lives had been torn apart. Their mother Farahild had died years earlier, and now their father was gone. What would become of them?

The two brothers naturally turned to Pippin for advice, who was Waldo's godfather after all, and now responsible for his godson's wellbeing.

Ruthard, now 20 years old, was taken in under the protection of his friend Warin's family and his future as the Count of Aargau was assured.

As for Waldo, Pippin knew that on the day of the christening, his godson had been promised to the Church. It was now time for Waldo, at 14 years of age, to begin his anointed duty of joining the clergy to provide for the spiritual welfare of his family.

"I have something for you, Waldo," Pippin said, taking a small box from his tunic. "Your dear father left it in my keeping. He knew he was dying before you left for Ravenna and wasn't sure he'd be here when you returned."

Pippin handed the box to Waldo who watched it intently as it was placed in his outstretched palm. He opened the box and instantly recognised his father's golden ring with the deep blue gemstone.

For Waldo the blue of the stone was the most magnificent colour he had ever seen and he had admired it from the first moment he saw it with those golden specks that shimmered like tiny stars.

"In the Arab lands, Waldo," his father had said, "this glittering blue gemstone is thought to have magical powers."

Fighting back tears in front of Pippin, Waldo slowly and reverently placed the ring on his biggest finger. It was too large but he knew he would grow into it soon enough.

"The gemstone is a Lapis lazuli," Pippin said. "It was your father's talisman. Lapis lazuli, because of its blue colour, has been regarded throughout history as the stone of friendship and truth. It is said to encourage harmony in relationships and help its wearer to be authentic and give his opinion openly."

It was a time of crushing sadness for Waldo. On top of his unbearable grief for his lost father, he was now faced with separation from his dearest friend, Charles. They had been inseparable since they were infants sharing the breast of Anneliese, and now, with childhood barely over, they were going their separate ways.

At first, Charles was more angry than sad.

"Why do you have to go into a monastery?" he demanded, fighting back tears. "You can come and be a soldier with me. I'm sure my father would allow it."

"No he won't, Charles," Waldo said quietly, trying to calm Charles who was very agitated. "He cannot. He is my godfather. He was present in the sight of God at my christening when I was promised to the Church. He cannot defy God's wishes, even if he wanted to."

Charles dropped his head in defeat.

"I know," he said, almost under his breath.

"We are best friends, Charles. It will never be otherwise. Our bodies may be in different places, but our hearts and souls are inseparable."

"We are brothers forever, Waldo," Charles said. "Let us swear to that, on the names of Anneliese and Othmar."

"And Nazarius and Celsus," Waldo added.

11

Bloodbath

Something Othmar once told him about fear had suddenly returned and taken up residence in Waldo's mind.

"The oldest fear," Othmar had said, "is the fear of the unknown. We all dread the darkness of the forest."

Waldo's future now seemed to him like a dark forest. He envied Charles who was born to be a soldier and a leader. 'Was I born to be a monk?' It was a question he had begun to ask himself on a daily basis. 'Who am I to be a saviour of men's souls?'

Pippin had ordered that Waldo enter the Benedictine Abbey on Reichenau Island at Lake Constance. As he prepared his belongings for the journey to Reichenau his doubts overwhelmed him. He wished desperately that he could have talked about it with his father. Richbold would have known what to say to him to ease his anxiety.

How would he cope with life as a monastery novice - virtually a servant - with no possessions, after living in a castle as the son of a nobleman? He suddenly felt much younger than his 14 years and the tears ran down his cheeks as he realised how much he missed his parents. He had never felt alone before and he found he had no way of dealing with it.

Despite his fears, however, he was determined not to let Charles see that he was afraid. His friend had come to see him in an excited state.

"Ruthard, Warin and I," Charles said, "are going to accompany you all the way to Reichenau!"

Waldo was secretly overjoyed at this news, but he controlled his reaction and kept it to a simple smile of appreciation.

"Thank you, Charles. But it's a very long journey – there and back. It's not necessary for you to come. It's arranged for me to travel with some monks who are returning to Reichenau from Strassburg."

"I will not let you head off into the unknown, into the darkness of the forest, without me."

Waldo stared at his friend, astounded, but said nothing. He was totally focused on fighting back the tears he could feel welling up behind his eyes.

"You're not the only one who remembers things Othmar told us," Charles said. "I was listening too, you know. He also said fear of the unknown is man's oldest fear. So it's alright for you to be afraid."

Charles paused, searching for the right words. "Othmar is a very wise man. He also told us that the future is a blank slate, a tabula rasa. We can write our own destiny on it."

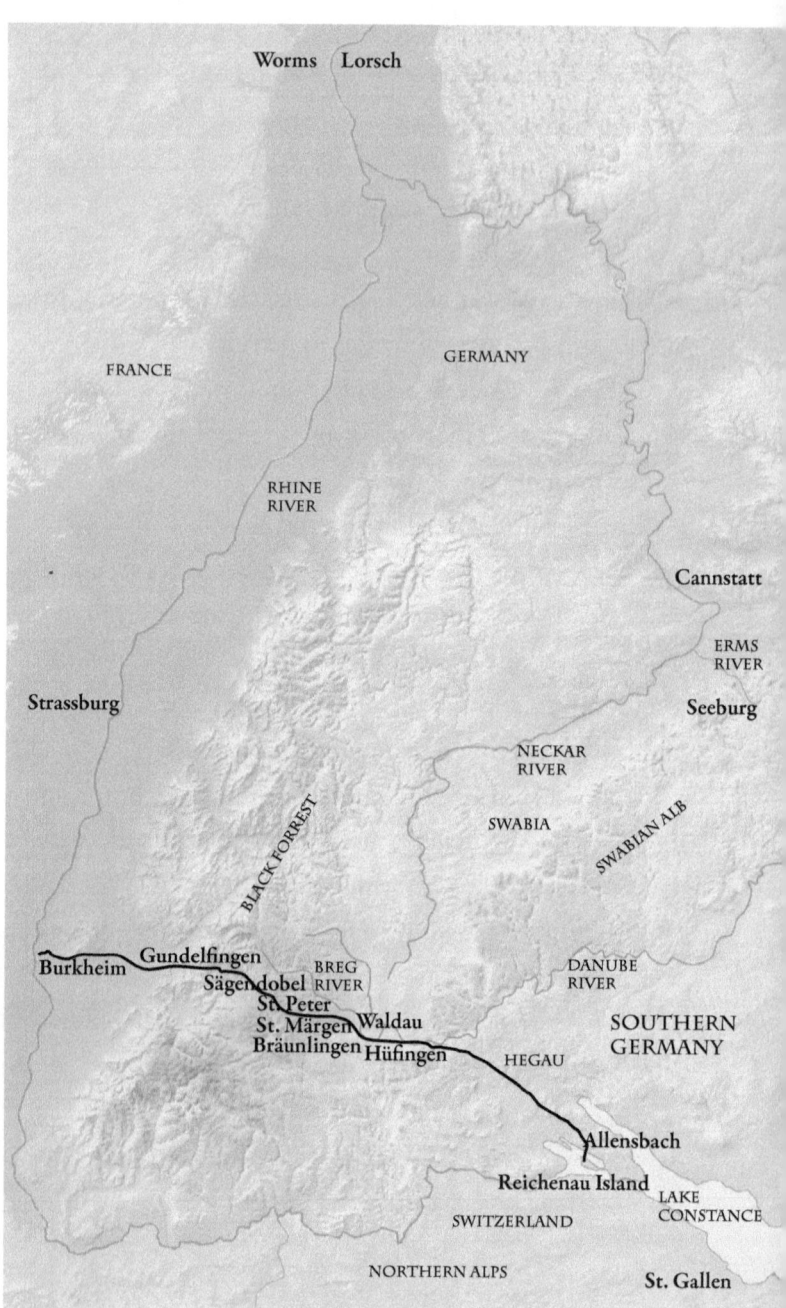

"Yours is already written, Charles."

"So is yours, Waldo my brother. You will be Europe's most powerful bishop."

†

Waldo was acutely aware of the long, hard path he would have to tread before he ever became an ordinary bishop, let alone the most powerful one in Europe. It wasn't hard to imagine what being a Christian missionary meant in the pagan stronghold of Swabia.

The Swabian Alemannic forests were full of pagan tribes who believed in cult rituals and feast days, celebrating sun dancing, tree worship, or blood sacrifices on mountain tops. Christians were few and far between in those godforsaken barbarian lands. Fortunately, Waldo reminded himself, there were also some people scattered around the region who weren't necessarily hostile to Christianity, so perhaps he could practise on them before tackling the pagan barbarians.

His first long, hard journey on his path of destiny, was from Burkheim on the river Rhine at the southern edge of the Black Forest, down to the Island of Reichenau at Lake Constance. As he studied the arduous route they would take on the simple map Charles had laid out before him, he thanked God that his friends were travelling with him.

"The first night of our journey," Charles was saying, "we will stay overnight at Gundelfingen. Next morning we will head off to Glottertal and spend the second night in nearby Sägendobel. After breakfast up to St. Peter and St. Märgen. We'll have a short rest at St. Märgen and then travel a little further up the hill to Waldau, see, they've already named a village after you Waldo! Then it is downhill along the Kaltenbach Creek and up the forest to Schwärzenbach. The next day we will continue on to Bräunlingen. Our family has friends there who will provide us with food and shelter, and we will stay overnight with them, and get a good rest."

It was all sounding quite matter-of-fact the way Charles was explaining it, but Waldo was already feeling exhausted. Maybe I was born to be a monk and not a soldier after all, he thought.

But once on the journey Waldo surprised himself, and Charles, with his fitness and endurance. When they reached Charles's friends' place at Bräunlingen, he was already beginning to feel like a missionary.

He knew enough from Othmar's teachings about Christianity to tell the family who had taken them in for the night, all about the martyrs who were willing to die for Jesus, the Son of God. They were so impressed with him that they begged him for more Christian stories. Their enthusiasm gave him confidence and his fears about the future started to fade.

As he farewelled his generous hosts the next morning, Waldo strode forward with renewed energy and began to look forward to his new life at the monastery.

†

"Look, down there, Waldo," Charles said, pointing to a thin strip of river disappearing into the trees. "That's an early stretch of the mighty Danube, but they still call this river the Breg. A little further on is our next stop, Hüfingen."

"There are old Roman baths there," Ruthard said. "We can have a good wash."

The baths were a welcome treat for the weary travellers and all four of them romped around like children for some time. A while later, Ruthard and Warin decided to see if they could find the ruins of an old Roman fort called Brigobanne.

"This town used to mark a boundary of the Roman Empire," Warin said, as he and Ruthard wandered off.

"We'll wait for you here," Charles said.

Waldo was deep in thought and Charles remained silent too.

"This would have been an awful journey," Waldo

finally said, "if you weren't coming with me ... and Ruthard and Warin too, of course."

Charles just shrugged as if to say, what are friends for?

"Your presence has given me confidence and helped me prepare myself for life at a monastery."

"Your uncle is the Abbot at Reichenau," Charles said. "You'll be privileged."

"No, it will probably be the other way because he won't want to be seen to be giving me any special treatment. He has already made it clear that I will be starting at the very bottom rung of the ladder."

"What will your duties be?"

"To begin with, those of a humble servant with no possessions. Not speaking until I'm spoken to; waiting for the other monks to eat before I can; holding a candle while others are reading; waking everyone up during the night for prayers."

"It will build character!" Charles declared, echoing the words his father Pippin had said to him on many occasions.

"I am prepared to try my hardest, Charles," Waldo said. "But I hope I have the strength of will to succeed."

"Well, the fact remains," Charles said, thumping Waldo on the back, "the Abbot is still your uncle, Pippin is still your godfather ... and I'm still your soul brother. So if you falter and fall, you have some good and powerful friends to help you up."

†

The next day the four travellers reached the Hegau, a spectacular landscape with many volcanic outcrops that had burst up from the earth millions of years before - lava explosions now frozen in stone. The breathtaking views stopped the four friends in their tracks and they paused for a considerable time to enjoy the magnificent panorama before them.

"Look there, Ruthard!" Warin announced, pointing at a huge mountain of rock and forest towering above them, dominating the landscape. "Up there would be a great place to build a fortress."

"We will keep it in mind," Ruthard said, laughing. "The Warin Ruthard Fortress of the Hegau!"

"Look, Waldo," Ruthard said, pointing to a distant speck of water to the south, "there's our destination, Lake Constance."

Waldo was both excited and saddened by the sight of Lake Constance. While it was the place where his new life would begin, it was also the point where he and Charles would part company. Perhaps it would be the last time he would see his friend for many years. He wondered if Charles was thinking the same.

He glanced at his friend who wasn't looking towards Lake Constance but beyond it to the majestic mountains of the Alps. Charles turned and smiled at Waldo.

"We crossed those Alps together, Waldo," he said. "Our greatest adventure. I will never forget that time."

"Nor me."

Charles and Waldo clasped both hands on each other's shoulders.

"Brothers forever!" Charles declared.

"Brothers forever!" Waldo replied.

They released their grasp of one another and stood in silence, contemplating the extraordinary vista before them.

"In a few days, down there," Waldo said, nodding his head towards Lake Constance, "we will say farewell and go on our separate journeys. It will be a sad day."

"Yes," Charles said. "But our paths will cross many times. And even apart, we will be working together for the glory of Europe and Christianity. Me the soldier, you the priest."

"The sword and the cross," Waldo said.

Charles drew his sword from its scabbard and held it aloft, waiting for Waldo to respond. Waldo reached under his cloak and took a small brass crucifix from a pocket in his tunic and held it aloft. They touched the cross and sword together.

"The sword and the cross!" Charles said.

They exchanged the two so that Charles held the crucifix and Waldo the sword. They touched them together again.

"The cross and the sword!" Waldo said.

Though both Charles and Waldo were unaware of it, Ruthard and Warin were watching the two friends' cross and sword performance, and they smirked at one another.

"You two little boys wouldn't know a real sword if you fell over it," Ruthard said maliciously.

Charles was still holding his sword.

"That sword of yours is just a toy, Charles."

Charles flushed and glared angrily at Ruthard, but Waldo jumped in to calm things down.

"What makes you and Warin such great warriors?" he said.

"We've seen real battles!" Warin declared hotly.

"What, from half a day's march away," Charles threw back, "peering from behind your bodyguards?"

"We were at Cannstatt when your uncle Carloman massacred several thousand Alemanni noblemen," Warin said, "for high treason."

"He didn't massacre them!" Charles shouted angrily. But deep inside he knew Warin was right. He had heard terrible stories about the Blood-Court at Cannstatt. It had wiped out almost the entire Alemanni tribal leadership.

Waldo was trying to find a way to take Charles's side.

"How could Carloman's men kill several hunderd armed noblemen without getting killed or wounded themselves?" he said.

"The Alemanni nobles didn't have weapons because when Carloman called them to the council they had to leave them outside," Ruthard said.

"They still could have fought back, or run outside and retrieved their swords," Waldo said, frowning.

"Apparently when the killing began the nobles were all too sleepy or groggy to do anything to defend themselves," Warin said. "During the feasting beforehand they must have been poisoned."

Probably with mandrake, Waldo thought to himself. It was a powerful poisonous plant he had learnt about from Othmar. With his incredible memory, Waldo could recall every word his beloved tutor had told him about mandrake. 'It was much used by the Ancients,' Othmar had said. 'They considered it a sleeping herb. In large doses it is said to excite delirium and madness. They used it for procuring rest and sleep, convulsions and pains. They extracted it from the bark of the mandrake root, either crushing the juice out of it, or infusing it in wine or water.'

"It is possible they were given a sleep-enducing herb in their drinks," Waldo said, looking apologetically at Charles, who was still red-faced and furious.

"Whether it was the right thing to do or not," Ruthard said, "it ended the independence of Alemannia and brought it back into our Frankish Empire. It was a brutal act, but it probably saved the lives of thousands of Frankish fighters in future battles they didn't have to fight."

This thought seemed to mollify Charles somewhat and he nodded, still scowling fiercely. A little while later, out of earshot of Ruthard and Warin, he asked Waldo which poisonous herb his uncle Carloman would have used.

"I think it was the sleeping herb called mandrake," he said. "Do you remember Othmar telling us about it?"

"Yes, you use the roots," Charles said. "But if you pull the roots out of the ground the wrong way, or the wrong time of day, the plant cries out."

Waldo had forgotten that, but he wasn't surprised Charles had remembered it. He had the kind of mind that retained stories of pain and violence.

12

Farewell

The ferryman was already waiting for the travellers on the shore of Lake Constance when they reached Allensbach. Waldo could see the Abbey on Reichenau Island just a short boat trip away. As they all clambered aboard the ferry, Ruthard couldn't resist having some fun at Charles's expense.

"Are you coming out to the island with us, Charles?" he said, grinning and winking at Waldo. "Or would you rather wait here for us?"

Ruthard hadn't forgotten Charles's terror of the small wobbly boat Richbold took them on to an island in the Rhine river near Alsace several years before.

Charles gave Ruthard a surly look, but said nothing, as he stepped onto the ferry.

"You will be much more comfortable spending the night at the abbey," Warin said, laughing and punching Charles on the arm, "than at the ferryman's hut."

Ruthard and Waldo's uncle, the Abbot of Reichenau, greeted them joyously and lavished on them all the comforts the abbey had to offer.

"But don't expect this tomorrow night, Waldo," he said warmly, wrapping an arm around his nephew's shoulder.

"Tomorrow you start as our newest novice."

Later that evening, after a fine meal in the refectory, Charles led Waldo down a long corridor to a quiet place he had found.

"This is the scriptorium," Charles said.

He placed a wrapped package on one of the monk's writing desks.

"I have a parting gift for you," he said, leaving his hand resting on the package. "But before you unwrap it, I have some things to say to you, Waldo."

Even as an infant, Charles had been full of nervous energy. Waldo remembered Bertrada saying on several occasions that she could never hold Charles in her arms for long because he would twist and squirm like an agitated cat until she put him down.

As Waldo watched Charles pace to and fro preparing what he wanted to say, he saw how tall and willowy his friend was getting. He hadn't noticed it before. Charles was still only just a teenager, but he moved with an easy, fluid grace. He had none of the awkward clumsiness of most young boys his age, including my own, Waldo reflected ruefully. Charles was rapidly turning into the lean and powerful warrior he was destined to become. Anatomy is destiny, he thought.

The phrase had popped into his head, but he couldn't remember where he had heard it. His sudden recollection of information or events was beginning to happen on a regular basis and Waldo wondered if he had been blessed with a special memory. Perhaps I am destined to be a sorcerer like Taliesin, he thought happily. What a team Charles and I would be then – the warrior king and the sorcerer priest! Being able to cast spells would be a great advantage in converting pagans!

The future warrior king had now stopped pacing and stood regarding Waldo with hands on his hips and a scowl on his face.

Waldo felt that Charles was scrutinising him from head to toe. His instincts were true.

"I am worried about you, Waldo," Charles said. "You are slim, and growing tall, but you are awkward and often clumsy. I have noticed that you are also forgetful of small, everyday matters that one must attend to in life. I know you have a fine memory for the scriptures and the many things Othmar taught us. But you seem to wander around in a bit of a daze. I only say these things because you are my dearest friend ... my soul brother."

Friendship and truth, Waldo thought caressing the blue gemstone ring of his father's that he now wore on his own hand. "This will be my talisman too my beloved father," he murmured under his breath.

"Friendship and truth, Charles," Waldo said still caressing the gemstone. "That will be our secret motto from this day forth. We must always be honest and open with one another and never afraid to express our opinions, no matter how confronting – as you have just done."

"You are not offended, Waldo?"

"I would be offended if you had thought it, but not told me."

Charles smiled and Waldo saw it as the smile of someone far older than Charles's tender 13 years.

"Friendship and truth is a powerful motto, Waldo ... and we will need all its power. We are soul brothers, but we are different."

"Our difference will test our friendship to the limit."

"If we are honest with each other even the hardest test will not break it," Charles assured his friend.

Charles had started to pace again. After several minutes he stopped and sat down opposite Waldo, looking highly agitated.

"You have to promise me, Waldo, that truth will never destroy our friendship!"

For a moment Waldo thought Charles looked more like a frightened young boy than future warrior king.

"Promise Waldo. Promise!"

"Calm down, Charles," Waldo said gently. "What's going on? Why are you so agitated?"

Charles was finding it difficult to look at his friend.

"I saw your face the other day on our journey here ...

when Ruthard and Warin told us about the bloodbath in Cannstatt. You weren't just horrified, you were also disgusted. I don't want you to ever be disgusted with me!"

"But you would never slaughter helpless people, Charles. I know you wouldn't – you couldn't."

"When I am king," Charles said quietly, "I don't know what I might have to do to defend our empire and protect Christianity."

"Implicit in friendship and truth, Charles, is trust. It is true that you will have to be a hard, sometimes even ruthless leader in battle - but I trust that you will never be a butcher of helpless, unarmed men."

"Like my grandfather and father, the Lord God has put me on earth to build and defend Christianity. He will expect me to do whatever it takes. This is not a gentle, benevolent God we are working for, Waldo. He may want me to do things I won't like doing, but it will be out of my hands."

"That would be most convenient for you Charles," Waldo said angrily. "You could be a brutal, bloodthirsty killer of innocent women and children and not feel responsible for it. *God made me do it*. If that ever turned out to be the truth, Charles, then it would break our friendship."

"Then I should defy God?"

"If the good Lord asks you to be a brutal murderer of the innocent, then He may be testing you Charles, like He tested Abraham when He asked him to sacrifice Isaac, his own son."

"I will never be a butcher like Carloman. I don't want the words on my tombstone at Saint Denis to say: Here lie interred the remains of the Carolingian Emperor Charles the Butcher, or Charles the Bloodthirsty."

"You and I are different, Charles," Waldo said. "God gave you a sword to do His work, and you must wield it to ensure loyalty and obedience, or Christianity is doomed. The Lord gave me a cross symbolising Jesus' crucifixion to inspire compassion and love for the faith."

"We are not so different, Waldo," Charles said. "We are just taking people on different paths to the same heavenly gates."

Charles tapped the package he had brought for Waldo several times with a forefinger, then gestured for Waldo to unwrap it. From the wrapping Waldo withdrew a large, flat rectangular object the length of his arm. It was a relief sculpture in terra cotta graphically depicting the birth, crucifixion and resurrection of Christ.

Waldo was overcome with the beauty and symbolism of the artwork and briefly could find no words to say.

"I thought it would look good on the wall of your monk cell," Charles said.

"It is the most beautiful artwork I have ever held in my hands," Waldo finally said. "It is the perfect gift. It will be the first thing I see in the morning and the last thing I see at night for the rest of my days."

Charles beamed with pleasure. "I found it in Mantua, it is by Antonio Jardi, an Italian sculptor who devotes himself to religious art."

"And I have a gift for you too," Waldo said, handing Charles a package small enough to hold in the palm of his hand. "I had it made by a silversmith in Burkheim."

Charles unwrapped the package and held up a shiny silver medal attached to a chain. He immediately recognized the symbol etched out of the medal's surface as a clever form of his Latin name, *Carolus*, that Othmar once sketched for fun using a 'K' for the Germanic *'Karolus'* as the first initial:

"Ah, Waldo ... you kept the sketch!" he said, admiring the silver medal glittering in the candlelight. "A special memory of our beloved teacher."

He kissed the medal and placed it around his neck. "I will make it my official insignia and shall carry it with me till the day God calls me," he said.

The two friends embraced in silence. There was nothing

more to say. But both were thinking the same thing – friendship and truth.

When Charles and Waldo said their farewells the next morning, they both knew that truth would severely test their friendship in the violent and brutal years to come as Charles became ruler and followed his destiny to Christianise Europe by the force of the sword.

Waldo could see already that Charles had no faith in the power of the cross to convert the barbarian pagans – that only the power of the sword could achieve it.

What Waldo couldn't see was that his childhood friend would become one of the most celebrated warrior kings in history, Charles the Great, the legendary Charlemagne. For himself, Waldo could see a very different path to the same destination of a Christian Europe – the path of the cross.

He fervently hoped their paths would meet many times because he loved his friend deeply. At the same time he feared that the conflict in their hearts would rip that love asunder.

13

Incarceration

It was well known that the Bishop of Constance was feeling jealous and threatened by the Carolingian dynasty's growing support of Othmar, and the praise he was receiving for his success as the first abbot of the Abbey of St. Gall. Othmar was also seen as a monk of the people by building an almshouse, a hospital, and the first leprosarium in the region.

When word reached Ruthard and Warin that the Bishop of Constance was trying to build a court case against Othmar, they saw their opportunity to finally bring down the man they had hated since their childhoods. They successfully plotted with the Bishop to bring false accusations against Othmar.

As young and influential noblemen by this time, their testimonies against Othmar persuaded the judges of the court that he was guilty of the charges brought against him. They accused him of having an inappropriate relationship with the wife of a local nobleman.

As a monk, Othmar was forbidden to have a relationship

with any woman, but having it with a married woman was an even more evil sin and serious crime.

Unfortunately for Othmar, the Sin of Lust was the worst of the Seven Deadly Sins to be accused of. Women were seen as vessels of the Evil One. Only Satan himself would have the power to tempt a holy man like Othmar, so he was therefore a disciple of the Devil, and doomed.

The other six Deadly Sins were Gluttony, Envy, Pride, Greed, Wrath and Sloth. All serious enough transgressions against God, but for the Church, Lust was worse than all those six put together. Othmar could have been a greedy, jealous, proud, angry, lazy glutton and escaped the wrath of the church and courts. But as a fornicator he was the Devil incarnate and all his past holiness and charitable works counted for nothing.

How ashamed and ridiculous the courts and clergy who sentenced Othmar would have felt if they'd known he would one day be declared a Saint.

Othmar was innocent of the false accusations, but his fate was sealed by the malicious lies of Ruthard and Warin, endorsed by the Bishop of Constance. Fortunately for the judges and clergy, vengeance and cruelty aren't Deadly Sins and they were able to sleep peacefully in their silk and satin sheets.

There was no peaceful sleep ever again for Othmar who was pronounced guilty and exiled to the small island of

Werd in the westernmost part of Lake Constance, and left there alone to starve to death.

Othmar's unjust and untimely death tested Waldo's belief in the Lord God. He began to doubt his faith and recalled the sneering words of a pagan nobleman he had met, who said to him: 'Faith is believing something you know isn't true.'

Soon after Othmar died, Waldo wrote a letter to Charles, but he never sent it to him. In the letter, he questioned God's love and mercy:

Living the life of a saint will ensure an eternity in Paradise after death, but it is no guarantee life on earth will become any easier as age wearies you. It seems that once God has decided you will be a saint, he turns his attention elsewhere and you're on your own, until you meet him in heaven.

Our dear Othmar will one day be recognised as a saint. But over the past year he was alone and suffering terribly.

I would have forgiven him for thinking that the Lord had forgotten him completely. Othmar wouldn't have thought that, of course. But I don't have his strength of faith. How could it be that of four students, you and I loved and admired him, and Ruthard and Warin hated him enough to want him dead, and to help bring it to pass. Where was God then?

(Othmar was canonised a saint about a century after his death by the Bishop of Constance. Perhaps the bishop was making restitution for the sins of his predecessor, the Bishop of Constance, who a little more than a 100 years earlier, had played a part in the shameful incarceration and ultimate death of the sainted Othmar.)

†

Waldo knew that Othmar would be praying constantly for an end to his ordeal, but the Almighty seemed not to be listening. The doomed abbot's plight tormented Waldo's waking hours and haunted his dreams in his cloister across the water on the Island of Reichenau. But he wasn't Almighty God, just a humble novice monk who had yet to learn the secrets of miracles, which is what it would take to save Othmar's life. Nonetheless, he decided he must do something to try and help him.

Unlike his friend Charles, Waldo had no fear of boats and water. As a novice monk at the abbey on Reichenau Island, he had occasionally rowed a small wooden boat the abbot used for an abbey-blessing ceremony conducted on the water a short distance from the abbey walls.

He had seen similar wooden boats moored on the

shoreline opposite Werd Island that were never used at night. His plan was to take a large bag of food out to Othmar in one of those boats.

There were no guards on the island but they occasionally patrolled the accessible parts of the lake shoreline, so he would have to plan his boat trip carefully.

14

Confrontation

Ruthard seemed obsessed with Othmar and his incarceration. Warin, on the other hand, was satisfied that Othmar was now exiled and as good as dead, and he showed no more interest in the doomed monk.

But Ruthard couldn't let it go, and sometimes, when the opportunity arose, he wandered on the shore of Lake Constance looking across the short expanse of water to Werd Island.

Some nights he would sit for an hour and stare towards Othmar somewhere out there in the darkness. Why? Surely he couldn't be gloating about an old man starving to death on a lonely island.

Waldo now saw his older brother Ruthard as a stranger and had not spoken to him since he had falsely accused Othmar of adultery. As he nervously pushed the small rowboat through a clump of reeds in the dark, it was the darkness in his soul that concerned him more.

He was now a novice priest dedicated to a life of Christian virtue and charity, but a hatred of his own brother was taking hold in his heart. He asked God for the strength to overcome it.

Clear of the reeds, in waist-deep water, he clambered into the boat and began rowing towards the island. His plan was to leave the bag of food for Othmar without seeing him.

He couldn't face Othmar because the grief and sadness would be overwhelming, and because he knew, that ultimately he couldn't save the abbot's life. He didn't know how many times he could bring food to the island – but he intended to do it as often as possible.

When he reached the island, he pulled the boat into the muddy shallows and dragged it up onto a dry patch of reeds. He tied the bag of food to a low-hanging branch and unwrapped a pitch torch he had brought with him. He jammed the shaft of the torch into the ground and lit it with flints.

The bag of food was clearly visible in the glow of the torch flame. Splashing through the shallows into the reeds, he quickly pushed the boat back into the water and clambered aboard.

As he rowed away facing the island he hoped that Othmar would see the torch and come down to the shore to investigate. After a few more minutes rowing, he thought he saw a figure moving around near the torch and prayed that it was Othmar and that he had found the food.

The burning torch caught the attention of another figure sitting in the dark on the bank of the lake staring out at the island. He jumped to his feet and ran down to the water's edge. In the flickering light of the torch on the water, he caught a glimpse of the silhouette of someone in a small boat, then it was gone.

Waldo was rowing as fast as he could away from the light on the water towards thick reeds near the shore, unaware he had been seen. Once in the shallows, he dragged the boat onto a patch of rocky shoreline and tied it to a large stone.

As he prepared to leave, he saw several sparks of light in the darkness close by. A small torch burst into flame and seconds later he could feel the heat of it on his face. He shielded his eyes with one hand and stepped back a few paces, almost stumbling into the boat he had just tied up.

"What are you doing brother?" a familiar voice hissed at him. "Are you trying to save that sad old man?"

"You!" Waldo exclaimed.

"This is treason, brother," Ruthard said. "You are defying Church and State by visiting that island. But I won't report you ... this time. You will bring shame on our family name."

"Shame!? Me?" Waldo cried. "Your lies and corruption have already shamed our family! You have destroyed everything our mother and father lived for. You have dragged their memory through the mud and filth of the pig sty that is your own life!"

Ruthard lashed out with the torch in his hand and tried to strike Waldo across the face with it who threw his hands up to protect himself. Ruthard dropped the torch and smashed his fist into Waldo's jaw, knocking him backwards against the boat. Dazed, Waldo tried to fight back as ferociously as he could. But Ruthard was bigger, stronger and a seasoned fighter. He struck Waldo several more vicious blows before leaving him slumped semi-conscious across the bow of the boat.

A faint glow of pre-dawn light was just touching the clouds on the horizon as Waldo managed to drag himself to his feet and start the painful walk back to Reichenau.

15

Missionary

The memory plays strange tricks on a troubled and exhausted brain. As Waldo laid down to sleep the night after his confrontation with Ruthard, one part of his conscious mind was recalling his brother beating him senseless. Another part was remembering the secret thrill he felt sneaking food out to Othmar alone, by boat under cover of darkness.

It occurred to him that it would have been a great adventure for him and Charles when they were still young boys. Despite the sharp pain it caused in his jaw, he couldn't resist a broad smile at the thought.

He wondered how Charles's training as a future military leader and empire ruler was progressing. Tomorrow his own serious training as a missionary monk began and his days as a novice ended. He needed to get a restful night's sleep in preparation and closed his eyes trying to put his encounter with Ruthard out of his mind, and instead focus on happier days when he and Charles were boys living a life full of fun and adventure on the Breisgau.

But sleep was elusive, and anything but restful. Whether it was a dream or one of his visions, Waldo couldn't tell. Suddenly his mind was assailed by a rapid series of images of Charles as an adult warrior king. The images flashed passed as if he were running along a corridor looking at pictures hanging on the wall as he ran by. Then they slowed down until he was left with just the one image of Charles near a river, seated on his charger surrounded by his army.

He was holding his sword aloft in one hand and pointing with the other to a vast gathering of barbarian men kneeling on the ground, heads bowed, like prisoners. There seemed to be several thousand of them. He also heard sounds - terrible sounds of men shouting, some giving orders and others crying out in terror.

The words 'Death to the heathen Saxon murderers! Behead them all in the name of Almighty God!' rang out above the din. Charles's men walked among the kneeling prisoners, swinging their weapons and decapitating them as they went. Many prisoners scrambled to their feet but they could do nothing to defend themselves because their hands were bound. Whether standing or kneeling, they were beheaded brutally and mercilessly. Many tried to run but were quickly cut down.

The blood-soaked ground became a gruesome tangle of decapitated corpses, scattered heads and frenzied soldiers, and all the while, Charles sat impassively on his charger observing the slaughter with a regal detachment. Then he turned and called out, 'Waldo! Come and join in

... we are converting the pagans!'

Waldo cried out in his sleep so loudly that it brought one of the monks running to his aid.

He shook Waldo gently, waking him instantly.

"You were having a nightmare, brother," he said, "there was a witch in your dreams."

Thank God it was just a dream! Waldo thought.

"Thank you brother," he said, "I am fine."

He knelt by his bed and prayed until weariness overcame him. He laid down on his bed and drifted into a deep sleep, this time, as originally intended, dreaming of himself and Charles at the Breisgau, running in the meadows and playing hide and seek in the forest.

†

Next morning, the refectory was still in darkness, lit only by candles and torches, when Waldo and ten fellow novices finished breakfast and headed to the scripture room for their first lesson in the ways of a missionary.

Their tutor was a missionary monk and teacher visiting from a monastery near Strassburg. He had been trained in the Christian faith by Saint Pirmin, who founded the abbey at Reichenau Island - the very abbey where he was now teaching young missionary trainees. And the tutor wasn't to know that the bruised and battered face among the eager trainees in front of him, belonged to a future Abbot of Reichenau Abbey.

Waldo was doing his best to ignore the pain in his face as he listened attentively to the tutor introducing himself.

"Good morning, holy brothers," he said. "My name is Brother Rüdiger. The name comes from a combination of two High German words, hruod and ger, meaning fame and spear. Hruodger ... now Rüdiger ... 'Spear of Fame'. I like to think of it as meaning the most famous spear in history."

The tutor had noticed Waldo's facial wounds, and pointed at him: "You, bruised brother," he said. "What do you think the most famous spear in history might be?"

"The Spear of Longinus." Waldo answered. "The lance that pierced the side of Christ on the cross."

"Exactly!" the tutor said. "Wielded by a soldier called Longinus."

He looked around at the faces peering up at him.

"So, as missionaries, let us think of ourselves as spears of the fame of Christ - wielding them to pierce the stone hearts of heathens with His glorious message of divine redemption for their sins."

He could have said for redemption of sins the heathens didn't yet know existed, but he didn't want to confuse his trainee missionaries with such complex theological issues too soon. The broad, basic teachings were sufficient for beginners.

"The Irish monks," he continued, "like St Columbanus and St. Gall, called their missionary way, *perigrinatio*, which means to wander or travel. We are on a mission - from the Latin *missio*, a sending. You will be sent on a wandering mission to convert the pagans to the ways of Christ. There is no more worthy calling on earth than the one you have chosen."

The tutor waited for his last comment to sink in before continuing.

"So, how do we teach the pagan barbarians to believe our beliefs? Why should they change the beliefs that have sustained them for many thousands of years?

First and foremost, belief is reality. I'll repeat that because it is the basis of everything. Write it on your slates in big letters – BELIEF IS REALITY. It doesn't matter what the truth or reality actually is, it's what people believe it is that matters. For instance, all of us here believe that God exists, but we don't know if it is true or not. We just choose to believe it. So for us, God is a reality.

Remember, heathens are simple folk, so when it comes to teaching them the holy scripture of the Christian Church, we must use one of the most powerful motivations, fear of punishment.

Heathens love myths and legends, so we must give them simple stories about the Word of God. The writers of the Bible and Gospels told interesting stories with a moral message, called Parables, which they believed were the actual words of Jesus.

I'm sure you still remember famous parables, such as the Prodigal Son, Good Samaritan, Seed Growing Secretly, Thief in the Night, Annoying Neighbour and so on. And of course, there were all the stories you loved about the saints and martyrs.

So you see, we didn't need any convincing to become Christians. We didn't have to think about it or make any decision - we were already learning to be Christians because we were growing up in a Christian home and society. As children we just enjoyed listening to wonderful biblical stories and parables and believed what the clergy and our parents told us about God and Jesus, and the Saints and Heaven and Hell."

Deep down, Waldo knew this was true, but he liked to think that now, no longer a child, his Christian beliefs and values were founded on something more intelligent and substantial than childlike innocence and wonder. It occurred to him that it was going to be much harder to convince people who hadn't been brought up as Christians, to suddenly believe in Christianity.

It worried him that the real truth was that priests and

monks were under the illusion they were missionaries doing God's holy work when they were nothing more than propagandists for the Church and state. Something else that troubled Waldo even more was his growing suspicion that the Church secretly, but happily, accepted the idea that missionary activity could be promoted by violence rather than spiritual means.

He knew what Charles's attitude and approach would be. Like his grandfather and father, Charles's simple solution would be to force pagans to accept Christianity with threats of retribution if they refused.

Waldo totally disagreed with Charles's approach. He didn't think people should be forced to accept Christian beliefs. But isn't that exactly what the Church is doing by threatening people with the torment of the everlasting fires of Hell if they don't believe? It can't be much of a religion, Waldo thought, if you have to use fear to convince people to accept it. They should want to embrace it through free will, not fear. So that would be his approach.

As if he had been reading Waldo's thoughts, the tutor turned to the topic of fear.

"The Church fathers," he said, "knew that persuading very simple folk to stop worshipping the magnificent wonder of nature and bow instead to a supernatural supreme being they couldn't see, would be extremely difficult. They knew that the only human emotion strong enough to do it, would be fear ... and not just fear, but man's oldest and most fundamental fear. And what is that? Does anyone know?"

Waldo knew. But he held his tongue in case one of the other novices knew.

When it was clear none did, he spoke up: "The fear of the unknown," he said. "The fear of the dark forest."

The tutor stared hard at Waldo for several seconds, as if he was trying to peer into his soul. Then he smiled and clapped his hands loudly together.

"Excellent! Very impressive, young brother," he declared jovially.

Although Waldo didn't know it at the time, but his tutor did, *the fear of the unknown was the invisible foundation on which Christianity was built.*

"Even though they are not nearly as clever and creative as we Christians are," the tutor continued, "pagan scholars are very cunning and can be very convincing. So, your first motto as trainee missionaries is 'Know thy enemy'. For tomorrow's lesson, I want you to identify some pagan beliefs and symbols that we Christians have borrowed and used against them. We must be prepared for the battle for the minds and souls of our enemies. As missionaries, we must defeat the heathens for the glory of Almighty God."

Waldo could now see that he and Charles weren't so different - both were going into battle for Christianity.

The cross and the sword.

16

Symbols

The morning's lesson had left Waldo with more questions than answers. But he knew that there would be many more questions, and doubts, he would have to confront and resolve before he could be a successful missionary priest.

He spent all afternoon, between prayers, in the Abbey library and applied himself diligently to the tutor's instruction to consider the relationship between Christian and pagan symbols.

He praised God that he was in a monastery and had the rare privilege of access to written knowledge and scriptures. Each day, more books and manuscripts were finding their way to southern Europe from Muslim Spain, and Waldo was hungry for any new knowledge he could get, Christian or pagan.

Waldo began his research with the most recognisable Christian symbol, the cross. He discovered that the cross was used as a pagan symbol thousands of years before Christ. The Vikings revered the cross as a sacred icon depicting the destructive hammer of Thor, their god of thunder and war.

The cross was also a symbol of one of the enemies of

God – Tammuz, a sun-god of ancient Babylon. The ancient letter Tau, the initial of Tammuz, makes a very clear cross. Burial urns displayed a symbol known as a sun cross – a circle around a cross. It was the Celtic cross, symbol of the pagan druids.

It was clear to Waldo that pagans first brought the cross symbol into the Church, which later adopted it as the cross of Christ, becoming Christianity's most powerful symbol. The more he learnt about the cross, the more he realised that much of Christian symbolism was based on ancient pagan sun-worship. And why not?

The sun was the oldest and most powerful god from the dawn of man. So it made sense that the Church should adopt symbols the pagans were already familiar with as its own. It was a clever and successful tactic by the Church, surreptitiously selling people new ideas under the guise of familiarity.

Perhaps the Church's most effective strategy, Waldo decided, was one that he himself saw being put into practice. When a new Christian church was being built to help convert barbarians, it would be erected on a known pagan site of worship, such as where a sacred tree once stood, for example, close to a sacred spring, grove or on top of a mountain.

Waldo was able to make a simple list of some Christian symbols and words adopted from pagan images and beliefs:

Cross. There are many pagan icons from various ancient sun-worship cultures depicting a cross.

Fish. Greeks, Romans, and many other pagans used the fish symbol before Christians. Hence the fish, unlike, say, the cross, attracted little suspicion, making it a perfect secret symbol for persecuted believers.

Halo. Greek halos, the ring of light around the sun. More sun-worship.

Easter. From 'Eoster' or 'Eostre' who was the Teutonic or Anglo-Saxon goddess of the rising light of day and Spring.

Holy. From 'holly', which was considered a sacred plant to Pagans.

Sunday. A Christian religious day – from 'sun day' of pagan sun-worship.

Madonna and Child. An iconographic image borrowed from the ancient Egyptian image of the goddess Isis nursing the infant Horus.

Noah's Ark. From the ancient Babylonian legend of Xisuthros, whose 'ark' came to rest atop a mountain following a global flood.

Christmas. Saturnalia was a pagan festival of gift-giving and feasting to celebrate the northern hemisphere's winter solstice. This solstice celebration was forbidden by the Church, but it didn't take much to tempt Christians to join in, which they did. So the church provided an alternative festival at the same time of the year in honour of the birth of Christ and called it Christmas.

Combined with his information about the pagan history of the cross, Waldo decided that his brief list of other examples was enough to satisfy his tutor.

"Well done, Waldo," Brother Rüdiger said the next morning. "Your list clearly shows that many pagan rituals and festivals were adopted by Christianity."

He studied Waldo's list again briefly, before continuing.

"Constantine and the bishops at the Great Council of Nicaea in 325 AD," he said, "organised and defined the Christian religion in terms of a Creed. And then three centuries later, Pope Gregory the Great – the Father of Christian Worship - set down rules for Christians to live by, based on the Creed of Nicaea."

Now, only a century and a half after Pope Gregory had lived, here he was, Waldo son of Richbold, about to embark on a life as a Christian missionary to teach the great Pope's rules and rituals to the pagan barbarians.

After vespers that evening, he went to the chapel alone for additional prayer and devotion to ask God to give him the faith and strength he would need for the formidable task ahead.

Reichenau, April 8, 764AD

17

Exams

The Abbot of Reichenau's voice rang out clearly from the pulpit, filling the church with Easter's joyful declaration of resurrection and redemption:

"On the third day He rose from the dead in accordance with the Scriptures."

A group of monks seated below him in the choir sang out as one:

"God has released His son from the torture on the cross and made him victor over death. The Magdalene has seen Him alive at the tomb and witnessed the wounds from the nails, spear and crown of thorns. The risen Christ says to her: 'Holy are those that don't see but still believe. I have the power of heaven here on earth and shall remain with you to the end of the world.'"

"Amen!" responded the congregation.

The Abbot surveyed the mass of faces before him. The Easter worshippers had packed the nave to overflowing and many were standing in the aisles. He waited until the church was absolutely silent. When it was as quiet as Jesus' tomb, he spoke:

"This is a very special Easter," he announced. "In 50 days time, 11 of our novices, including my own nephew, I'm happy and proud to tell you, will be ordained as priests and missionaries. They will be going forth to spread God's Word in the furthest corners of this land to convert the non-believers."

"I want to leave them with the image of a particular covert to Christianity, Paul of Tarsus, also known as Saul. Soon after Christ's resurrection, on the road to Damascus, Paul of Tarsus converted to Christianity when he saw a vision of Jesus. He ceased persecuting Christians, followed Jesus and later he became one of Christianity's foremost missionaries as Paul the Apostle."

The Abbot turned to face the 11 novices, who were lined up in front of the altar rail, and addressed them directly.

"Holy brothers," he said, "there is no better inspiration for you than a non-believer and persecutor of Christians who not only converted to Christianity, but chose to work as a missionary converting others. Go forth on your own Road to Damascus with my blessing in the sight of the Almighty Lord God."

†

The spring air over Lake Constance was alive with birds

and insects. Its cool freshness invigorated Waldo and his ten companions as they marched at a brisk pace along the lake's southern edge towards their destination, the Abbey of St. Gall. With the Abbey visible in the distance, the group stopped briefly for refreshments. As he munched on a juicy carrot and gazed at the great monastery up ahead, he couldn't help thinking of Othmar. If this journey was five years earlier, he thought, it would be dear Othmar who would be greeting me at the Abbey gate. Waldo closed his mind off to distressing images of Othmar starving to death on Werd Island, and instead recalled the many happy days he and Charles had spent learning wonderful new things from their beloved tutor. In my mind, you are already Saint Othmar. One day a Pope will declare it to be so.

Despite the sadness in his heart, memories of Othmar also excited Waldo because part of his final training as a missionary priest at St. Gall's Abbey would be gaining special knowledge of Othmar's herbal medicines. As a boy he had loved learning about plants and herbs from Othmar and now he would be discovering his deepest and most precious herbal secrets.

As the group started walking again, a novice called Theo suddenly stopped and pointed excitedly at the ground a little way in front of him. He was pointing at a large, flat stone with a depression in it that looked remarkably like the imprint of a human foot. They all gathered to study the footprint frozen in stone.

"See there," Theo said. "Perhaps it is the imprint of Jesus' right foot as he left earth and ascended into heaven!"

"If it were so," Waldo said, laughing, "we could build our own monastery on this spot and we would have pilgrims flocking here from all over the world."

"We wouldn't need to be missionaries – they would come to us!" said another novice, Jonas, getting a laugh from everyone.

The group was in a cheerful mood as they got nearer to their destination. All were excited about this last stage of their training. They had about 30 days of secret learning ahead of them where hidden knowledge of essential missionary skills would be revealed to them. They would learn herbal healing of the sick, survival skills for living off the land, and techniques to grow their own fruit and vegetables. And they would be given the seeds required. After that they would be ordained as priests and ready to set out into the world as missionaries.

"Once our final training here is finished," Theo said, "we must hurry back to Reichenau for Ascension Day. Like Jesus with his Apostles, we must take a last supper with our teachers."

Ascension Day is 40 days after Easter, Waldo

reminded himself. And then there is just one more official duty before we can finally go out and do what we are trained for - to spread the Word of God.

"50 days after Easter," Jonas said, as if he were breaking into Waldo's thoughts, "we will be ordained by the Bishop of Constance on Pentecost Sunday."
"And then we can get on with it!?" Theo asked, with mock frustration.

"Then we get on with it, at last!" Waldo said exuberantly, reflecting the collective confidence and enthusiasm of the whole group.

As they all headed off for the final leg of their journey to the Abbey of St. Gall, Waldo silently thanked Othmar for the knowledge and inspiration he had given to two young boys all those years ago.

18

Enlightenment

For Waldo, each day of his final training at St. Gall was an intense but exhilarating physical and intellectual adventure. He gained practical expertise, as well as extraordinary knowledge, learning many of the hidden - and forbidden - secrets of nature.

On the practical side, he had learnt a variety of many fundamental but useful skills required for the missionary life, such as farming, harvesting crops, and animal husbandry. He discovered the satisfaction of growing grapes and producing wine, preparing food and cooking it, and making and repairing garments.

He marvelled at the medical instruction he received, and the insights into reading, writing and arithmetic and also the arts, especially singing and drawing. He was amazed at the skill of the St. Gall scribes who demonstrated the art of copying manuscripts and illuminating the books of the Scriptures. And his tutors revealed an entirely new dimension to his understanding of theology and philosophy and the deeper, more powerful meanings of the Bible and the Scriptures.

For Waldo, learning the psalms was a particular challenge, he didn't have a musical ear and worked diligently all his life improving his singing and chanting.

But he was an enthusiastic and natural student in meditation and he found it a great comfort after a day of less than inspiring singing and chanting.

†

Perhaps the most challenging and confronting new knowledge revealed to Waldo and his friends Theo and Jonas, was in the mystical and magic arts, the practice of which was forbidden by the Church. They were introduced to the ways of the alchemists, the conjurers and the hypnotists.

As astonishing and challenging as their final training was, nothing prepared them for the last few days. One early morning immediately after lauds, the abbot led them down a long staircase deep into the bowels of the monestary. A hundred steps later they finally reached the bottom and entered a vast cavernous chamber. The novices found themselves standing in total darkness, not sure what they were supposed to do next.

As well-disciplined trainee priests, none spoke and waited patiently for instructions from the abbot. They stood silently for several minutes without a sound being heard, except for their own breathing. Suddenly a huge door slammed shut in the blackness behind them, the noise reverberating throughout the vast space, which acted like a huge, stone echo chamber.

Each of the 11 trainees almost jumped out of their skins, simultaneously, but still none spoke.

The next thing they heard was a man's voice, not the abbot's. It was quiet and deep, but crystal clear as it resonated throughout the chamber. It was impossible to tell where the voice was coming from.

"Brothers," the voice said. "There are demons here among you."

The voice stopped, replaced by strange sighing and hissing sounds that swirled around the trainees, who instinctively huddled closer together in the blackness. Apart from a few sharp intakes of breath, all maintained their silence. As the sighing and hissing sounds grew louder, the trainees felt small gusts of air on their cheeks as if the demons were brushing against them as they swirled around. The trainees sought each other's hands out in the dark and stood together as one gripping each other tightly.

After what seemed an interminable time, the sighing and hissing ceased. The trainees were emotionally spent, and some were on the verge of fainting. At that point a spark flashed in the darkness and a single torch flared into life. As the flame settled and burnt without the slightest flicker, it illuminated the figure of a man standing beside it. He was tall and elderly, with a long white beard and shoulder-length white hair. His robes glistened in the torch light.

"Brothers," the figure said, with the strong, clear voice of a much younger man. "I have tested your nerve, and it has not been found wanting. I am impressed by your courage and discipline."

Several more torches were lit by unseen hands and the trainees were able to see one another again. Their collective relief that none of the group had been carried off by demons, was palpable.

Waldo could see the mysterious figure more clearly and sensed an otherworldly aura about him.

"You will need all the courage and discipline you can muster to successfully perform the skills I will teach you here over the next few days. You will learn how to ward off demons and evil spirits, and exorcise those possessed by the Evil One."

Like the rest of his fellow trainees, Waldo felt a shudder through his entire body and found himself both fearful and excited about the lessons to come.

"You will also learn of the hidden secrets of nature," the mysterious figure said, "knowledge so extraordinary that you will think it is magic. Some so powerful and wondrous that it is forbidden to those outside the clergy. The forces of nature are usually dismissed as beyond man's capacity to understand. I will show you they are not."

The speaker paused, blessed himself and picked up a bowl of holy water. He dipped his hand into the bowl several times and flicked water droplets over the assembled trainees.

"My name is Aureolus," he said. "I am not a sorcerer, but I am different. Let this not disturb you. I can tell you that I have not bartered my soul with the Devil to obtain forbidden knowledge, as some have said. But what I cannot tell you is how I came by such knowledge. Heed my words and take away what you can understand. But be warned - do not try to practise what you don't understand. And whatever you do, never attempt to commune with demons if I am not present. Evil spirits live among us. They will not harm us, as long as we ignore them. To try to contact them means certain death, in the most horrifying circumstances."

The trainees were listening so intently it seemed they had stopped breathing.

"Let me tell you a story," Aureolus said. "It is about the terrible fate of a former pupil of mine, called Konrad. One night when I was conducting business rather late into the night, Konrad entered my chamber without permission to study a book of incantations that summoned demons. Opening the book at a particularly quick and effective such incantation, he recited it aloud. Perhaps it was beginner's luck, all bad in this instance, but he inadvertently caused a demon to appear there and then, whereupon, poor Konrad died of fright on the spot."

"I happened to arrive back at my chamber just as the doomed youth collapsed dead on the floor. Because most people fear what they don't understand, I knew immediately that I would be suspected of killing the poor boy. The demon had fled as soon as it saw me, but I called it back and compelled it to enter and reanimate Konrad's body. It did as I commanded, enabling Konrad's corpse to walk several times around the courtyard outside so that people who saw it would assume it was still alive. Eventually the demon fled and the body collapsed, but I was absolved of any blame."

Waldo and his colleagues were transfixed. They were torn between awe and terror of Aureolus. Each made his own silent oath that he would not attempt to summon a demon under any circumstances, with or without Aureolus's presence.

"Now, let us think about magic!" Aureolus declared exuberantly. "A wonderful, exhilarating topic ... if you have the mind for it. Unfortunately many men of the church, do not. They think magic involves satanic forces.

They are wrong! We live in a world where most clergy are like children – they think magic is evil and demons lurk in every dark corner."

Waldo wondered that Aureolus could say such things, to be critical of the clergy while speaking in a great abbey like St. Gall. But perhaps that is the point of our education, he thought. The more enlightened within the Church know these truths, but want to keep them secret from the ordinary people to use them to keep them submissive and obedient.

"They think magic is the mistress of every form of iniquity and malice!" Aureolus continued with renewed vehemence. "They say it lies about the truth and infects men's minds - that magic seduces them from divine religion and prompts them to the evil, corruptive, cult of demons. Again I say - they are wrong!"

"True magic is simply the use of the invisible forces of nature, such as those that draw certain metals together, and cause objects to fall to earth. Magicians do no more than hasten the hidden processes of nature ahead of time. This is natural magic - good magic that is consistent with Christian theology and entirely separate from the powers of the Devil. It is the use of true, natural causes to produce rare and wondrous effects by methods neither superstitious nor diabolical."

Waldo found Aureolus's words astonishing. The

idea that magic was real, and not a diabolical force was exhilarating to him. It helped him believe that what people called the supernatural, was real .... that God was real!

Aureolus was now walking among the trainees, introducing himself to each individually.

"Well now, brave young brothers," he said, "it is my turn to find out what you know about demons and magicians."

Their bravery apparently didn't extend to being the first to volunteer a display of their knowledge to Aureolus. They were all still in awe of him, and extremely nervous with him now among them. He could be a mind reader for all they knew. All were trying extremely hard not to have any thoughts strong enough for him to detect. Theo was the first to succumb.

"Yes, Brother Theo?" Aureolus said brightly.

He's remembered all our names already, Waldo told himself.

"I know that the poor often turn to magicians," Theo said "when they are ill or feel they have been placed under a curse ... or when they want protection from evil spirits, bad luck or pestilence. Where else could they go? Only a rich man could pay the healer's fees."

"And what does the Church think of that?" Aureolus said.

"It strongly disapproves," Theo answered confidently.

You are doing well, Theo, Waldo thought. Keep it up.

"According to the priests," Theo went on, "man suffers because of sin, and for that there is only one remedy: God's grace, which is what priests are there to dispense."

"The magicians also undercut the priests' trade," Jonas threw in, emboldened by Theo's confidence. "It robs them of the fees that the clergy can charge for their services. The Church tries to ease people's suffering with prayer, the magicians try with spells."

"We clergy can't have it both ways," another young priest chimed in. "We can't condemn magic and wizardry while at the same time encouraging our flock to believe in holy miracles. If you believe in miracles then you believe in magic."

Waldo finally felt inspired to say something.

"But if magic is simply the use of the invisible natural forces of nature, as Aureolus told us," he said thoughtfully, "then magic and miracles are different. Miracles may still be supernatural ... the work of God."

"Well, then," Theo said, rejoining the fray, " perhaps God is an invisible, natural force of nature as well. Perhaps nothing is supernatural at all."

Theo's idea seemed to have discouraged further comment and a confused silence prevailed.

"That is what the ancient ones, the pagan druids of the old way used to think," Aureolus put in with a broad smile, clearly delighted with the quality of the discussion.

"For them, Mother Nature was God. Through their mystical incantations they called on her to give them their power as healers and magicians to help the simple folk. And she heeded their calls."

"How are simple folk," Waldo said, "supposed to make a distinction, or a choice, between the incomprehensible Latin prayers of a priest and the mumbled obtuse incantations of a magician? If it's all gibberish to their ears, we might as well be magicians instead of priests."

"What we priests must do," Jonas said, "is convince the barbarians that our Latin prayers are us talking directly to God in his language, while the gibberish of magicians is them talking to Satan in his language."

"Excellent, brother Jonas!" Aureolus declared. "You are getting the idea. But do not dismiss the magicians too readily. Waldo is also on the right track. As priests, you can use the magicians tricks and illusions to persuade the unbelievers to believe in a supernatural God. We just need to be clever in our thinking and be open to opportunities – especially those provided by Mother Nature. Let me tell you about a trick I invented in Scotland and Ireland some years ago."

He gathered his cloak around him as if a chill wind had unexpectedly swept through the chamber.

"I heard about a long-forgotten legend," he said, as he began to wave his arms rhythmically above his head, "that people thought approaching storm clouds were a gathering of demons in the air. So I resurrected that legend and the priests and missionaries began to teach it throughout both countries. Then we told people that the only way to ward off the demons was to ring the church bells. If they didn't have a church we recommended they build one soon. Ringing the church bells worked of course, because during storms, no-one saw a single demon."

Aureolus paused and moved away from the group of trainees. He stepped up onto a raised area slightly above them. The silence in the vast cavernous chamber was deafening. He raised his arms in the air and held them there.

It struck Waldo that it was some kind of signal, so he steeled himself for a sudden shock or surprise. He was the only one of the 11 trainee priests who didn't jump with fright when it happened.

An incredibly loud crashing noise that sounded like thunder, echoed through the chamber. As it faded away, an enormous flash of intense green light lit up the dark space and they could all see just how vast and cavernous it was. The incandescence of the initial flash burnt out quickly, but a strong green glow remained that lit up the walls of the cavern and the thick cloud of smoke left by the green flash. Aureolus was gone, as if vapourised by the flash.

With his colleagues, Waldo watched the events with a mixture of excitement and fear. They saw the cloud of smoke rapidly grow in size and strength until it filled the vast space and enveloped them. It was like the thickest fog Waldo had ever encountered and he couldn't see his hand in front of his face. Once again, he heard strange sighing and hissing sounds and cool breezes swirling around him in the cloud. Suddenly the strange sounds ceased, obliterated by a second crashing of thunder. Seconds later it stopped and the vast chamber was once again filled with silence. Waldo also noticed that the thick cloud remained, but the green glow was beginning to fade. Soon he was in total darkness again and the sighing and hissing sounds and cool breezes had returned. He stood still for several minutes trying to stay calm.

His attempt was short-lived. When the loud ringing of church bells rent the air, he jumped and gasped aloud.

He wasn't alone - all novices had reacted in the same way.

Mercifully the ringing bells stopped one at a time until silence prevailed again. As the last bell faded into the distance, lit candles began to appear in the darkness and a bright warm glow soon filled the vast chamber. The air was clear, the smoke cloud gone.

Aureolus had gone too, but he had made his point. In reality, Christianity had nothing to offer the pagans that they didn't already have. But as Brother Rüdiger had taught him, Waldo knew that it didn't matter what the reality actually was, all that mattered was what people thought the reality was. For the Church, as long as people believed the idea of a supernatural God and heaven and hell, the fact that no-one knew if it was true or not, wasn't important. Belief was everything – truth was irrelevant.

Waldo realised that Aureolus was showing them that missionaries needed to be conjurers and illusionists; that tricks rather than truths were the secret to converting pagans.

For Waldo, as false as trickery seemed, it was still far preferable to the gruesome brutality of the sword.

19

Ordination

"The days run away like horses over the hills," Waldo said to Theo and Jonas. The three had become firm friends during their missionary training at St. Gall. Their last month of learning and instruction had rushed past and disappeared in a blur. It had exhausted Waldo and his colleagues emotionally and physically. But it was an exhilarating experience, and for each of them, it had ended all too soon.

"Where did 34 days go?" Waldo said, shaking his head in bewilderment.

"In less than half that time," Theo said, "in just 16 days from now, the Bishop of Constance will ordain us as priests."

A short time later, Waldo found himself sitting alone in one of the abbey chapels. For some reason he just felt the urge to find a bit of solitude and time to himself.

"I am to be a priest, at last," he murmured aloud, barely above a whisper.

An extraordinary quiet and stillness came over him, a dream-like tranquillity he hadn't known before. At that point he felt the shadow of his father's death withdraw. He could feel the heavy, stifling cloak of melancholy being lifted from his shoulders. Until now he had been following a vague, narrow path to a life in the Church, but suddenly it was a wide, clearly signposted road, well lit with torches on either side.

While he couldn't see exactly where it would take him, he knew with every fibre of his being that it was a road he wanted to be on for the rest of his life.

At daybreak the next morning, as soon as prime prayers were concluded, the 11 novices set off on their return journey back to Reichenau Abbey. They had done everything required to prepare themselves for the priesthood. As they walked out through the gates of St. Gall, each one of them was feeling proud of his achievement.

As usual, Waldo, Theo and Jonas stuck together as a group and chatted incessantly about the new knowledge they had gained. With their individual interests, they were impressed and excited by different things they had learned. But all three shared a fascination and awe of their mysterious tutor, Aureolus.

"Apart from his wonderful theatrics," Waldo said, "I learnt a great many things from him about pagans and paganism that I had never heard before."

"The best thing I learnt that I'd never heard before," Theo said, mischievously, "is the phrase: 'Happy as a Heathen.'"

He waited for a reaction, which was immediately forthcoming. Waldo and Jonas looked at him and then at each other, as if they couldn't believe their ears. When they saw the huge grin on Theo's face, they both burst out laughing.

"We'll have to keep that to ourselves," Jonas said. "If the heathens hear that, it will set Christianity back for centuries."

All three roared with laughter and were set upon by some of their travelling companions who demanded to be let in on the joke. Soon the entire group was chuckling away happily. It was a beautiful sunny day and there was good humour all round.

"Well, Waldo," Jonas said, smiling "what were you saying about paganism before Theo rudely interrupted?"

"It wasn't what I had intended to say," Waldo explained, "but the phrase happy as a heathen, reflects the pagan philosophy perfectly. Since about the 4th century the word pagan has come to have a Christianised stigma to it. Today it signifies a person who is sensual and self-indulgent, who cares only for earthly possessions. Someone who doesn't care about the future and isn't interested in a religion other than that of devotion to physical pleasure."

"Before the 4th century," Jonas said, "the word pagan didn't have any religious meaning. It was the Latin slang word 'paganus', which meant a country rustic or village dweller. A heathen was a rustic who lived on a heath."

"How are we going to turn people away from a belief in earthly pleasure and possessions?" Theo said, looking discouraged. "Convincing them to believe instead in spiritual joy on earth and a reward in an invisible supernatural place called heaven, won't be easy."

"But not impossible," Waldo insisted, "as the pale Galilean, our Lord Jesus has proven."

"And those pagans who die before they hear the word of God," Theo said, "are they condemned to the eternal fires of hell? Is ignorance a sin?"

"If you're not aware you're offending God," Waldo said, "then I'm sure He won't be offended."

"Then I suppose the pagans would be better off if they don't hear what we want to tell them. If they knew that, and saw us coming, they would run! Pagans can just keep enjoying an indulgent earthly life and still go to heaven."

"Yes," Waldo agreed. "But they will never experience the joy of the love of God while on earth, as we do. What good is sensual pleasure without spiritual ecstasy?"

Jonas and Theo had no answer to that and all three lapsed into their own silent thoughts about the inadequacy of mere pleasures of the flesh.

The three friends walked for some time without speaking, deep in contemplation. Waldo was so engrossed he gradually slowed to a stop and stood considering the religious life he had chosen, unaware that the rest of the group had continued on without him. After some time, he sat on a fallen tree trunk by the side of the trail and began to question, and finally doubt, his ability to convert pagans by the word of God alone.

"Perhaps Charles was right," he muttered to himself. "Perhaps it is a hopeless cause without the threat of the sword."

Realising he had fallen a long way behind the others, he stood up and headed off after them at a brisk walk. He hadn't gone far when the flash of sunlight off to his left, caught his eye. It seemed to have come from a shiny, metallic object he could see sticking out of a rock among some shrubbery on a rise about 40 paces away.

As he approached the shiny object he saw that it was a magnificent sword that seemed wrought from pure silver with an ornate, intricately worked hilt made of a second, darker metal. The weapon was wedged upright in a crevice in the rock.

Up ahead, Jonas and Theo had realised Waldo was no longer with the group and were on their way back to find him. They passed the spot where Waldo had left the trail to investigate the flash of sunlight and didn't see him standing among the shrubbery scrutinising the sword wedged in the rock. But they heard him.

Waldo reached out and gripped the hilt of the sword to pull if from the rock. The instant he closed his fist around it, he screamed out in agony. It was as if he had grasped the red-hot end of a blacksmith's poker.

A little further along the trail, Waldo's scream stopped Theo and Jonas in their tracks and they rushed back to where the sound had come from.

For Waldo, initially the pain in his hand was excruciating, but within several seconds of his grasping the sword, the pain miraculously and totally ceased. When he looked at the palm of his burnt hand, he gasped with astonishment.

There were no fresh burns or blisters, just a vivid red scar that looked as if it had been there for many years. It was in the shape of a cross, reaching from one side of his palm to the other. Studying the scar more closely he could see that it contained a darker shape within the overall cross shape. When he recognised the second shape he fell to his knees – it was in the form of the crucified Christ.

As he continued to stare at his palm, an intense flashing of light from the sword in the rock dazzled him and he held up his hand to shield his eyes. When the flashing light finally ceased, Waldo watched the magnificent silver sword disintegrate and fall onto the rock as small pieces of metal. A second later the pieces reformed into a small, ornate silver cross.

Waldo looked at it laying on the rock for some time, hesitant to pick it up after his painful sword experience. Despite his fear and bewilderment at what had occurred, he saw that the small silver cross was beautifully made. It was formed by two layers of silver metal and a third darker layer in the shape of a winged cross.

Eventually he reached out and picked it up gingerly with two fingers. To his immense relief, it was cold to his touch. He turned both his palms up, one held the silver cross and the other his miraculous crucifixion scar.

He was studying both in an almost trance-like state when he was jolted back to reality by the sound of Jonas and Theo calling out his name. As they reached Waldo, both realised something extraordinary and divine had happened to their friend. He was kneeling in the dirt and they saw he had tears in his eyes when he looked up at them. He smiled and asked them to kneel with him.

In a shaky voice, he told them he would later explain the miracle that had just occurred.

"For now," he said, "Let us give praise to the Almighty God of heaven and earth and look ahead to that wonderful Sunday two weeks hence when our dream of ordination will finally be fulfilled."

†

"Vi et animo", chanted the Bishop of Constance. "With heart and soul, and strength with courage, go forth in the Apostolic Succession and continue God's mission in Christ for the Church."

Waldo and his 10 fellow novices were kneeling with their foreheads resting on the Holy Table. Their hands were clasped in prayer and their feet were bare following the foot-washing ceremony only minutes earlier.

The bishop moved around the table laying his hand on the head of each novice in turn. He then stepped back several paces and spread his arms wide in a gesture that symbolically embraced the novices in the bosom of the Church.

"Sacramentum Ordinis," he said. "I ordain you with the sacrament of Holy Orders. In the name of the Father, Son and Holy Ghost. Arise now as priests of the sacred Church of Christ."

As each new priest rose to his feet, he held his hands out, palms upwards and the bishop anointed them with holy oil. He noticed Waldo's crucifix scar, and frowned, but made no comment.

"In your hands," the bishop said, "I place the gift of holy priesthood bestowed by our Lord God."

†

Later, once they had farewelled friends and family, Waldo, Theo and Jonas gathered together outside the church in the balmy evening air. Free to relax for the first time that day, the reality of their ordination finally hit them. As if on a secret signal, they simultaneously threw their hands in the air and cried out in unison: "Praise the Lord!"

As they congratulated each other with great vigour and excitement, Waldo wished Charles were there to share his success. He would be proud of me, he thought.

"Soon we go north on our first missionary walk," Jonas said with a sweeping gesture in that general direction.

Waldo's mind was already on the march. I will be walking north with my new friends, but my dearest friend, my soul brother Charles, will be at my side in spirit, every step of the way.

North

Charles's spirit was making its presence felt even before Waldo had taken his first step on his missionary walk.

His thoughts were firmly fixed on the many places north of St. Gall he would be visiting, across Lake Constance, over the Danube and beyond. So he was surprised to find his mind suddenly travelling back across the Alps to Ravenna.

A message from Charles just as Waldo was about to set off on his walk, instantly transported him to the magnificent octagon Church of San Vitale, named after Saint Vitalis. The vivid memories of his and Charles's visit there 10 years before, had never left him.

The real shock for Waldo though, was the way the message was delivered.

"Waldo!" the abbot cried, bursting in on Waldo, Theo and Jonas as they made their final preparations. "You have a special visitor!"

The three young priests looked at one another wondering what could possibly get the dignified Abbot of Reichenau so excited. He took a few moments to re-gather the dignity that had deserted him momentarily.

"The Imperial Bishop, Fulrad," the abbot announced

calmly, "the Abbot of St. Denis, has travelled all the way from Paris to see you, Waldo."

Theo's and Jonas's eyes fixed on Waldo with admiration and awe. *We've chosen the right friend here!* their eyes were saying.

Waldo was equally astounded, but he was thinking clearly enough to know that it had something to do with Charles.

†

An hour later, Waldo and the abbot were standing in the Chapter House awaiting the arrival of the Imperial Bishop. Behind them stood a welcoming party of monks and priests from Reichenau. The abbot's dignity seemed under threat again because he was wringing his hands nervously. Waldo was a little tense too, but he was also intrigued.

He was about to make a comment, when Abbot Fulrad and his entourage swept into the Chapter House.

"Welcome, your Magnificence," the abbot said, "to the Abbey of Reichenau."

"Thank you, Eminence," the Imperial Bishop said, extending his right hand for the abbot to kiss the Imperial ring. "The Lord be with you and all the brothers of your cloister."

Fulrad glanced immediately at Waldo: "You have grown up Waldo," he said, extending his ring hand once again. Waldo dropped to one knee and kissed the ring. "Congratulations on your recent ordination," the Imperial Bishop added.

"Thank you Sublime Lord Bishop," Waldo said, bowing his head.

Fulrad gestured for Waldo to rise from his knee.

"I understand," he said, "that you and the other ten new priests were exemplary students throughout your demanding final training process. Once again, the good Lord has chosen well and the future of God's missionary work is in good hands."

Fulrad glanced at the abbot: "I would like all 11 of the newly ordained priests to come forward so that I might congratulate and bless them individually."

On a signal from the abbot, Theo, Jonas and the rest of the young priests joined Waldo and knelt before the Imperial Bishop who spoke to each of them in turn and made a cross sign in holy oil on their foreheads.

After the impromptu ceremony, the Imperial Bishop singled out Waldo once again.

"To you, Waldo, congratulations also come from King Pippin and Prince Charles," he said, unrolling a small scroll. "The Prince has a personal message for you. He says: 'Waldo, remember our visit to the Church of San

Vitale in Ravenna? I will never forget it. Well, now you shall carry the holy remains of the martyr Saint Vitalis, after whom the church is named, to Esslingen at the river Neckar in Swabia. This as a favour for the King – and an order from the King too, of course.'"

He could see Charles smiling at that last part of the message: 'And remember too, Waldo, I will be walking with you in heart and spirit. Carry Saint Vitalis safely. Vi et animo - strength with courage.'

Waldo was overwhelmed with pride at the honour bestowed on him by King Pippin. "Vi et animo," he murmured under his breath. Holding his emotions in check, he vowed to all present that he would carry out his holy task with all the strength and courage he possessed.

Watching quietly from the back of the room was a young novice who had been appointed as Waldo's assistant on the pilgrimage walk. All the missionaries were assigned a helper who stayed with them for their entire journey and helped their master set up in whatever location he chose as a base for his missionary work.

As his assistant, Waldo had chosen a 14-year-old Swabian boy called Godsbert whose knowledge of the area and understanding of the Swabian dialect, would be of great value and advantage to the new, inexperienced priest and missionary from Reichenau Abbey.

As Godsbert heard the personal message to Waldo

from King Pippin and Prince Charles, delivered by the Imperial Bishop himself, he realised that his master was special and would one day be a great and important bishop. He also knew that he and Waldo would be venturing further and deeper into the Swabian badlands than any of the other missionaries.

Godsbert felt both honoured and anxious that Waldo had selected him. He was the second son of the Swabian nobleman Bertholdis who christened and named him with his vocation and family name. As the second-born son, he was donated to God – he was God's Bertholdis or God'sbert.

My father would be proud of me, he thought.

†

That evening, Waldo sought a private meeting with the Imperial Bishop. Fulrad was happy to indulge the godson of the king and dear friend of the prince.

"Thank you for seeing me, Sublime Lord Bishop," Waldo said.

Fulrad smiled magnanimously as he gave Waldo his blessing. "It is my privilege and pleasure, Father Waldo."

Waldo nodded his head in appreciation. "I am keen to hear news of Prince Charles and how he is progressing," he said. "I have not seen him for a number of years now."

"The prince is a most excellent and impressive man," Fulrad said, "a young lion. He is already a powerful and imposing figure, and a highly skilled fighter. He is taller than most men, as you are Waldo ... but the prince is stronger and more athletic I would say."

Waldo grimaced slightly. As a boy he was always described as scrawny, whereas Charles was seen as wiry. It was a distinction he couldn't see himself at the time.

"Prince Charles also has gifts of the mind equal to his physical prowess," Fulrad continued. "His constancy of mood is most admirable. He does not suffer fools, of course, but he is patient and fair in his dealings with all, and treats his mother Bertrada and sister Gisela with the greatest reverence."

"And his brother, Carloman?" Waldo said. "I have heard rumours that they do not like one another."

"It is Carloman's doing," the Imperial Bishop said wearily. "He is jealous of Prince Charles and constantly hostile towards him. Everyone is impressed with Charles's tolerance of his rancourous young brother ... and his determination not to be provoked to anger by him."

Waldo realised that Fulrad would give a glowing account of Charles and wasn't totally convinced of his friend's tolerance and patience when provoked. However, he knew he would still get a good idea of how Charles was developing from the Imperial Bishop's information.

"As a boy," Waldo said, "Charles was a keen student and eager to learn all manner of things. Is he still that way – or is his interest now all about weapons and war?"

"Far from it Father Waldo!" Fulrad declared vehemently. "He is learning the art of calculation, as well as rhetoric and dialectic. He is interested in astronomy and has investigated the path of the stars across the heavens."

The Imperial Bishop paused and raised his eyes to the vaulted ceiling, perhaps seeing past it into the vastness of space and the realm of heaven beyond.

Waldo too was staring into the distance following a fleeting thought of his own. He remembered Charles's fascination with the night sky from the time he was only two or three years old. He knew it was true of most children, but Charles seemed obsessively interested for one so young. He recalled with pleasure how he and Charles would sit for hours up in Richbold's tower in the dark making out different shapes formed by clusters of stars, such as animals, household items and weapons.

As he reminisced he realised that Fulrad was talking again.

"Prince Charles has even expressed the desire to learn to write. He has also decided that it is not enough just to speak in his native tongue, he is trying to learn foreign languages as well. He already knows Latin well enough to use it for prayer, and can understand and speak Greek."

Waldo smiled with pleasure that Charles was still passionate about his education beyond the ways of war. Othmar will be smiling down on him too, he thought.

Perhaps Fulrad was a mind reader because Waldo was startled to hear him use the old tutor's name.

"The Benedictine Othmar was a great influence on our Prince," Fulrad said, "as he was on you yourself, Waldo."

The Imperial Bishop smiled broadly at Waldo's look of surprise.

"Prince Charles has spoken often of his childhood tutor and how he inspired him and his friend Waldo to embrace knowledge and learning."

Waldo's mind instantly returned to those boyhood days when he and Charles hung on every word Othmar said.

"And you will be pleased to know, Father Waldo, that your friend Prince Charles is a devout Christian and practises his faith with great piety."

"My dear friend seems almost too good to be true, Lord Bishop," Waldo said mischievously. "Surely he has some weaknesses and flaws."

"Well, perhaps one," Fulrad said, chuckling "is that he sets such a high standard in everything that it can be intimidating for us mere mortal men to keep up. He is most restrained in his wine drinking and very much hates to see anyone drunk. But he is not so disciplined with his food, especially roast meat served on spits – this is irresistible to him. He believes fasting is bad for his health. Although he is in no peril of growing fat."

Like me, Waldo thought. No matter how much I eat, I remain like a string bean.

†

"Be mindful of the example of Boniface, God's great missionary," the Abbot of Reichenau said the next morning, the moment the bells for prime prayers had stopped ringing. "May his shining spirit illuminate the black nights and dark forests ahead."

The abbot was standing before the gathered missionaries with his arms outstretched in final blessing before they departed. Among the large group kneeling before him were monks, priests, assistants and the men-at-arms who would act as bodyguards on the hazardous journey through wild and brutal barbarian lands.

"Remember his readiness for adventure and eagerness to overcome difficulties in the service of the Church," the abbot continued. "Boniface applied his profound faith to religious devotion in distant and dangerous parts where he could forsake his family and friends and homeland for the sake of the Lord. His holy passion to convert the heathens was satisfied only by enduring long hardship as a good soldier of Christ."

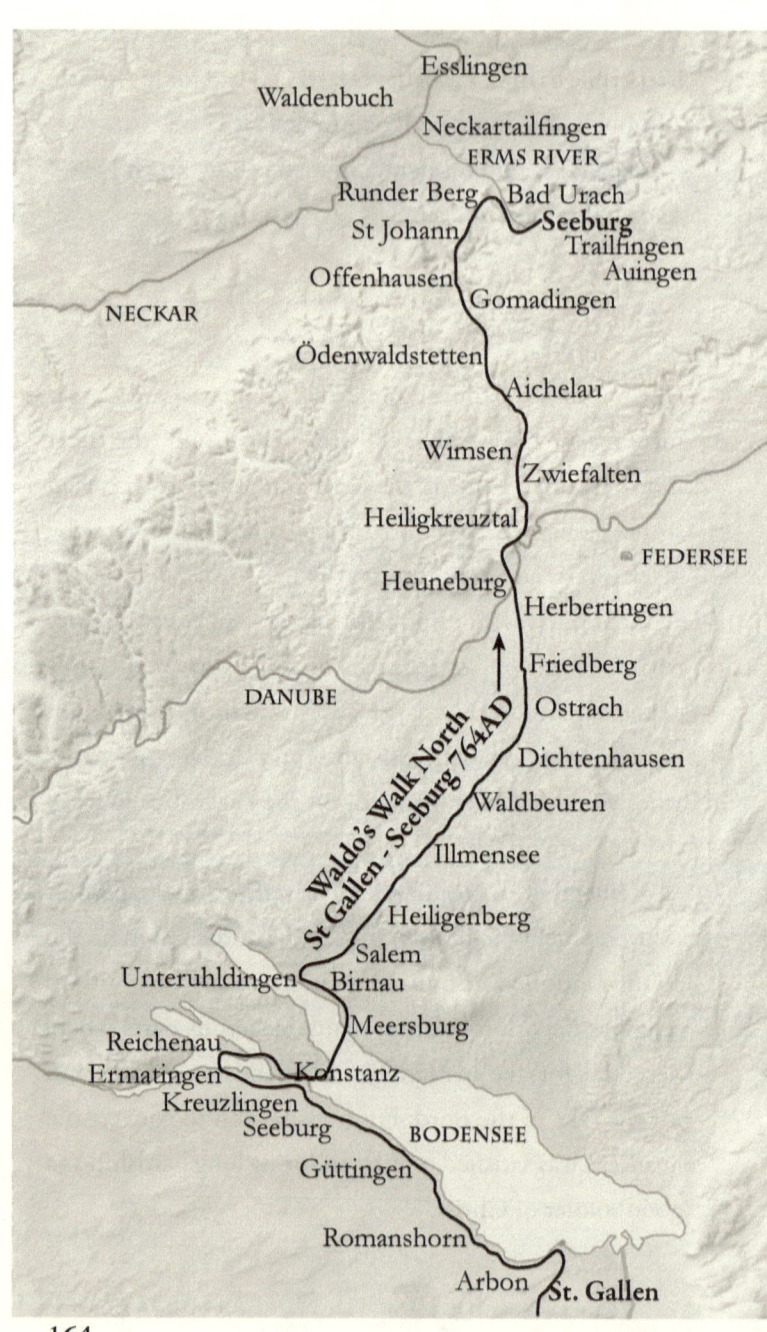

Esslingen

Waldenbuch

Neckartailfingen

ERMS RIVER

Runder Berg · Bad Urach

Seeburg

St Johann

Trailfingen

Offenhausen

Auingen

Gomadingen

NECKAR

Ödenwaldstetten

Aichelau

Wimsen

Zwiefalten

Heiligkreuztal

FEDERSEE

Heuneburg

Herbertingen

Friedberg

DANUBE

Ostrach

Dichtenhausen

Waldbeuren

Waldo's Walk North

St Gallen - Seeburg 764AD

Illmensee

Heiligenberg

Salem

Unteruhldingen

Birnau

Meersburg

Reichenau

Ermatingen

Konstanz

Kreuzlingen

Seeburg

BODENSEE

Güttingen

Romanshorn

Arbon · St. Gallen

The abbot made the sign of the cross over the gathered group: "Go forth my good soldiers of Christ," he cried out joyously, "and sow the seeds of salvation!"

Finally, we are on our way, Waldo thought as he made the sign of the cross himself, and kissed the crucifix hanging around his neck.

"Good soldiers of Christ," Theo said as the group filed out of the church. "I never thought I'd be joining the army!"

The cross and the sword. Waldo again thought of Charles. They were both soldiers in God's army.

With the rest of the missionary party, Waldo, Jonas and Theo assembled at the threshold of the great gates of the Abbey. They made last-minute checks that their belongings on the pack mule they were sharing, were securely tied. Waldo had two precious items that he had taken special care packing. He had wrapped the terracotta gift Charles had given him at Reichenau in thick wool padding covered with heavy leather. It hardly moved when he tried to jiggle it, and he patted it gently several times, satisfied it was safely packed. The remains of Saint Vitalis had already been carefully packed in a small iron relic box before they arrived at Reichenau. He had made certain the relic box was safe and secure.

As the missionary party moved out through the abbey gates, Waldo offered a prayer for his mother and father. He reminded himself that it was for the spiritual well-being of his family that he had been promised to the Church in the first place. Also, with a great effort of will, he said a prayer for the soul of Ruthard, asking Othmar's forgiveness at the same time. 'Dear Othmar, God has given me strength to retrieve the charity and love that I had buried deep in my heart to forgive Ruthard for what he did to you. I hope you have forgiven him too.'

†

About an hour's walk out from Reichenau, Waldo paused and looked back at the abbey where he had said goodbye to Charles and his training as a novice. He saw it as the first tile in the mosaic of his life as a missionary.

Theo and Jonas were also gazing back at Reichenau, lost in their own memories and emotions.

Jonas was the first to break into their reverie.

"Well that's the past," he said, turning away from Reichenau and pointing across the lake to some unseen place in the distance to the north. "And that's the future."

"Before we get to the future," Waldo said, with a laugh, "we will visit Constanz, which is very famous for its past. It used to be called Constantia, named after the Roman Emperor Constantine, who fought the Alemanni in these parts over 400 years ago. I think the past will follow us like a Roman ghost for a while yet."

"And some Celtic ghosts, too," Jonas said. "When we get to the upper Danube, around Heuneburg and Heiligkreuztal, there are Celtic settlements and hillforts from ancient times."

"Do you think you'll go that far?" asked Theo. "Some of the priests and monks are already talking of settling near Ostrach."

"That might be smart," Waldo said. "Godsbert tells me the forests between Ostrach and the Danube are very dark and forbidding places – full off barbarians and thieves."

"And wolves and bears," Theo added.

"The Lord will see us safely through," Jonas said.

"And we have our bodyguards in case the Lord isn't paying attention," Theo responded with a smile.

†

It seems the Lord was paying attention, at least until the missionaries reached the Danube. But as Godsbert quietly told Waldo, it was in the forests north of the Danube that they would need the Lord's protection more than ever.

Between Heiligenberg and the Danube many priests and monks had dropped out of the group and stayed behind at various points along the way. The group now numbered only 10 missionaries and their assistants. Theo and Jonas were still there, as well as three other young priests who Waldo had become friends with on the journey. They were Amadeo, an Italian priest from Salerno; Peadar, an Irish priest from Cork and Marcus, a French priest from a noble family near Poitiers.

When they crossed the Danube and reached Heiligkreuztal, Marcus and four others decided to remain there. The five remaining priests, their assistants and several men-at-arms pushed on further north through the forest to Zwiefalten.

Shortly after passing through Zwiefalten, Theo's assistant, a novice called Arnulf, stumbled over loose stones underfoot, losing his balance and falling down a steep rocky slope beside the rough path they were following close to Wimsen. Arnulf tumbled head over heels all the way to the bottom, before disappearing into some thick bushes at the edge of the forest. The unfortunate youth was crying out in pain as some of the others hurried down to help him as quickly as the rocky slope would allow.

Waldo was the first to reach him and found poor Arnulf covered in cuts and bruises with blood streaming from a wound on his head. Head wounds always bleed profusely and look worse than they are, he told himself. What concerned him more was that he could see that Arnulf had broken his right arm, and a massive, swollen bruise on his ankle suggested that he had broken or sprained that as well.

After a great struggle with much slipping and sliding, the rescuers managed to get the injured Arnulf back up the slope to the path.

"There's no break in the bones," Waldo said, after a close examination of Arnulf's ankle. "But his ankle is severely sprained and he won't be able to walk far on it for many days."

Medical skills, such as binding broken limbs, was part of every missionary's training and very soon Arnulf's broken arm and sprained ankle were bandaged securely.

Waldo called the other priests together for a crisis conference. Theo had already decided a course of action.

"Arnulf is my assistant," he said. "He can't continue on. We have only travelled a short way from Zwiefalten, so I will return there with him. I will make a walking crutch for him. It is too late in the afternoon to set out now. We will leave at first light tomorrow."

"I will accompany you," Amadeo said. "We can't spare a bodyguard. The others will need all the protection they can get as they go further north."

"We will camp here, in this small cave, for the night," Waldo said. "We still have about an hour or so before sunset to collect firewood ... and make some torches just in case we need to scare off wolves or bears. As well as their swords, our bodyguards also have bows and arrows."

†

Darkness arrives with a rush in the thick forest. Soon the black sky was a mass of glittering stars, unlimited layers of tiny lights stretching back to the edge of the universe. A large fire was blazing brightly, holding back the chill air drifting down through the trees.

The vast, unending sky crammed with countless heavenly bodies reminded Waldo of God's awesome power. Here, surrounded by great rocky crags and impenetrable forests, he felt himself in the presence of the Divine. Here, the line between the natural and the supernatural seemed less certain than elsewhere. Waldo was convinced that awesome, forbidding landscapes were those rare places on earth where one had a chance to glimpse the face of God.

As he lay back enjoying the warmth of the fire, it wasn't the face of God that he glimpsed in the branches of the tree directly above him. It was a face like he had never seen before, teeth bared, eyes glowing in the firelight. A savage face ... primeval and terrifying.

Waldo reacted instantly and rolled to one side towards the fire as the creature in the tree dropped to the ground with a cry like a wounded animal. The sound was a signal. Instantly, several more figures emerged from the trees and attacked the missionaries. The creature that had dropped from the trees rushed at Waldo, who had grasped one of the long torches he had made earlier. It burst into flame when he touched it in the fire. He turned just in time to thrust it at the barbarian as he lunged forward with a knife. Waldo could see the man's face was covered in a mass of black loops and curls - like tiny snakes - coiled around his eyes and crawling down his cheeks.

The burning torch stopped the barbarian in his tracks momentarily. It was enough time for Godsbert to bash the attacker over the head with a large lump of firewood from the stack they had piled up. The three bodyguards were fighting ferociously with their weapons, while the other priests and their assistants had followed Waldo's example and were waving flaming torches around trying to keep the attackers at bay. But more barbarians were emerging from the forest and it would be just a matter of time before the missionaries were overwhelmed.

Waldo ran over to a fallen tree trunk they had been using as a seat. He reached behind it and grabbed an extra large torch he had made just before he lay down to sleep by the fire. He also pulled a white linen hood over his head, like a small sack with eye holes cut into it. He ran back to the fire and thrust the large torch deep into the flames.

When he withdrew it, the torch blazed brilliantly illuminating the entire clearing with an intense bright green light. Waldo strode around the clearing holding the torch over his head emitting a loud, high-pitched moaning sound as he did so.

The whole weird effect with the strange coloured green light, Waldo's white mask and the eerie noise he was making, frightened the barbarians. It frightened the assistants and bodyguards too, until they realised it was Waldo and not a visitor from some supernatural realm.

The barbarians looked around at one another in confusion and then began to melt back into the forest.

Waldo left his mask on and kept the green torch alight until it burned out. In the meantime he made another green torch in case he needed it before dawn, which was still five or six hours away. He and one of the bodyguards stayed awake for the rest of the night while the others got some sleep.

†

The night passed without further attacks and the group started on their way in the pre-dawn light. Two of the bodyguards had suffered knife wounds in the attack, which the priests were able to effectively clean with herb infused hot water, then bandage.

"That was an incredible performance last night, Waldo," Godsbert said. "It had me fooled for a second!"

"It was a trick they showed us during final training at St. Gall," Waldo said. "It was developed by Boniface, as a defence for missionaries against barbarians, who are very simple and superstitious. Boniface was the most skilful and inventive missionary of them all. The very intense green flame is caused by a special powder, which is a mixture of certain dried herbs and saltpetre – also called the secret salt."

"Amazing!" Godsbert said. "And what were those marks on the barbarian's faces last night?"

"They are stains under the skin, called tattoos," Waldo said. "To make them look more fearsome and ferocious. Some of the barbarians adopted it from the Romans who used to tattoo the foreheads of slaves, as well as thieves and other criminals. I urge you away from such a practice ... it is a very painful process requiring sharp, pointed implements to pierce the flesh."

"Amazing!" Godsbert said again.

"What's amazing is that we survived that attack," Jonas said, catching up to join them at the front of the group. "Thank you again, Waldo!"

"And thank Boniface, too," Waldo said. "And the good Lord of course."

"Peadar and I have decided to divert to Meidelstetten," Jonas said. "We will settle in that area."

"Well you have come further than all the rest, Jonas."

"Except for you, Waldo."

"I have no choice but to continue. As you know, I must deliver Saint Vitalis's remains to King Pippin's friend at Esslingen."

21

Rejection

Perhaps the word had spread among the forests north of the Danube that a strange sorcerer with green fire was travelling through and was best avoided, because the remaining missionaries reached Aichelau without further barbarian attacks.

Of course, the bears, boars and wolves of the forest hadn't heard about the strange sorcerer and his terrifying powers, so Waldo, Godsbert and the two guarding soldiers had numerous encounters with the wild beasts lurking in the shadows.

Now that they were such a small group, the forests beyond Ödenwaldstetten seemed more gloomy and impenetrable than all they had passed through before. Huge oak, pine and beech trees formed giant barriers, made more menacing and mysterious by the veils of dense fog and mist shrouding the landscape.

On most occasions when they were confronted by predators, the flames of the fire or the waving of torches was enough to discourage them. But one night around the fire a large and powerful intruder proved more difficult to scare off. The wild ox had crashed through the undergrowth and straight through their fire, scattering flaming wood and glowing sparks in all directions. The terrified travellers scattered too and hid behind large trees until the ox decided to leave.

Another time, a brown bear chased a wild pig right through the clearing in which they were setting up camp for the night.

Despite such near misses and lucky escapes, the small band of four intrepid travellers gradually made their way through Gomadingen, Offenhausen and to the Round Mountain near Urach.

"Look," said Godsbert laughing one morning. He pointed to some small white clouds appearing in between some trees, as if there was a fire burning. "The rabbits are cooking their breakfast."

"You know this region far better than any of us, Godsbert," Waldo said. "What do you think of this area as a place to set up our little church?"

"Anywhere in the vicinity of Urach would be most suitable, holy father," Godsbert said. "Very well," Waldo said. "We will go into Urach and get some food and drink, and a good night's sleep."

He waved his hand in the direction of a large dome-like outcrop silhouetted against the twilight sky in the gathering gloom.

"Tomorrow we will go up there to the Round Mountain and pay our respects to the local pagan warlord of the region."

†

Morning brought a cold, blue mist drifting down from the surrounding hills. Godsbert was well rugged-up against the chill when Waldo joined him as he was unloading various packages from the mule.

"Greetings, Godsbert," Waldo said.

"Greetings Father," Godsbert stammered, his teeth chattering with the cold.

"I have a dilemma," Waldo declared. "We cannot properly pay our respects to the barbarian lord without a gift. I have completely neglected to bring any such thing."

Godsbert looked down at the packages he had just unloaded, then bent down and picked up a wooden box. Packed inside, in straw, was a Roman terracotta bowl with distinctive ornament engravings at the rim.

"Would this do?" he said. "It is the beautiful bowl you brought with you from Burkheim. Perhaps we could fill it with food and offer it as your gift."

"Brilliant Godsbert," Waldo exclaimed. "That will do perfectly!"

Compared to what they had been through over their many weeks of travel, the trek up to the Round Mountain was a casual stroll. They were in good spirits as they approached the entrance to the warlord's fortress.

The guard at the threshold allowed them to pass and they were greeted in the entry hall by a sombre servant. With a curt dip of his head, he turned and led them through to the great hall, where the pagan nobleman sat with his wife and several advisers.

"Majestic Lord, " the servant announced, "Father Waldo of Reichenau Abbey, a Christian missionary priest, and his novice, begging your indulgence."

"Step forward, Waldo of Reichenau," the nobleman said, "and state your business."

"My Lord," Waldo said, bowing. "Please accept this bowl of food as a gift of goodwill."

The servant who had announced them took the bowl from Waldo and placed it on a small table beside the warlord.

"I am seeking your permission to build a Christian church here in Urach." Waldo said.

The pagan warlord's response was immediate and violent. He snatched up Waldo's terracotta bowl of food and smashed it on the stone floor at Waldo's feet. As it shattered, a large, jagged piece crashed into Waldo's left ankle, opening up a wide gash. He could feel the warm blood seeping down between his toes, but he didn't flinch.

"By the blood spear of Wotan – the great god of nature," the warlord bellowed, "we will have no house of the Christ in Urach! You and your Christians are not welcome here! Begone!"

Waldo bowed respectfully, and with a glance at Godsbert, who looked about to faint, he turned to leave. The warlord, still red in the face after his volatile performance, seemed to calm down somewhat.

Perhaps it was a grudging respect for Waldo's quiet dignity because the warlord had noticed the young priest's badly bruised and bleeding ankle.

"Waldo of Reichenau," he said, "We don't need your God, we have more than enough of our own. But you have my permission to go a distance up the river Erms near Seeburg at the bottomless lake and build your Christian temple there."

†

Waldo was not discouraged by the warlord's rejection. By morning his ankle had improved enough for them to set off towards Seeburg.

"At least we have his permission to build our church in the area," he said brightly to Godsbert in an attempt to cheer up his assistant, who was still dejected by the confrontation with the pagan warlord.

A short time later they came over the crest of a large hill, not prepared for the view below. They stopped and stared down at a beautiful lake.

"Look at that, Godsbert!" Waldo exclaimed. "That's a sight to lift your spirits!"

Godsbert was delighted: "Praise the Lord!" he called out exuberantly.

"This end of the lake looks like the perfect place for our church Godsbert." said Waldo.

And so it proved to be. Later, down by the shore of the lake, Waldo saw that his initial impression had been correct. The river was narrow and shallow providing an easy crossing for animals and carts. Even though an isolated outpost, it was already an important trade route crossing of the Swabian Alb.

Waldo could see the great possibilities of having a church near the crossing with its constant movement of people back and forth. There will be many new prospects for conversion to Christianity, he told himself. And the gentle, shallow waters will be perfect for baptising the converted.

"And we will have clean water to drink, Godsbert," Waldo said. "We are upstream of our nasty neighbours on the Round Mountain, so we won't be drinking water they and their animals have fouled."

Waldo was keen to begin building his church, but

first he had to fulfil his special mission to deliver the remains of Saint Vitalis to Esslingen. He was confident of the route he must take so he and Godsbert and the two bodyguards set off without delay. Their journey took them downstream the river Erms to Neckartenzlingen where it met the river Neckar. They then followed the Neckar downstream until they arrived at a river crossing that took them to the township of Esslingen.

News of their arrival had preceded them, and King Pippin's friend Hatti, a Christian Alemannic nobleman, welcomed them with great warmth and appreciation. He included Waldo and Godsbert in the celebration and ceremony of the relic transfer from Ravenna to Esslingen, via Waldo's missionary walk from the abbeys of St. Gall and Reichenau.

Though the numbers of Christians in the town were still small, they were growing rapidly, and every one of them was at the Saint Vitalis ceremony.

The noble Hatti, to whom the saint's remains were to be entrusted, invited Waldo to address the gathering.

"I feel that I have not just come from Reichenau with Saint Vitalis, but all the way from Ravenna," Waldo said. "Many years ago I visited the church of San Vitale in that beautiful city with my friend Prince Charles, son of King Pippin who was responsible for bringing the saint and martyr's remains to the safekeeping of his friend Hatti here in Esslingen."

"In my travels, I have seen amazing developments in art and learning. Recently I saw books written in liquid ink on sheepskin. Here on this holy occasion, I promise that one day, perhaps in more than one thousand years, a beautiful book will be written about this special place that will be remembered in history as one of the crucibles of European Christianity."

Led by Hatti, the people applauded Waldo heartily.

"And," Waldo announced, "I will soon establish a settlement in this region and will call it 'Waldenbuch im Schönbuch' - Waldo's beautiful book."

22

Belief

"We mustn't put the cart before the horse," Waldo said to Godsbert, who wanted to begin building the church at Seeburg without delay. "Your enthusiasm is most admirable, Godsbert, but we must first have a plan. We need to design our little church, choose a site on which to put it, and then figure out who will help us build it ... and when."

Godsbert could see the sense of Waldo's argument and reluctantly accepted it. He was familiar with the region and understood Waldo's last point very well.

"You are right, of course, father," Godsbert said apologetically, "I am just eager to start. We cannot get any workers and builders to help us until the end of harvest celebration on the first Sunday in October – until then, all able-bodied men and women with their children will be working full-time in the fields harvesting supplies for winter."

They both knew that immediately after that, the people gave thanks for the bountiful harvest in a sacred ritual. It was the time to slaughter some animals and eat heartily to put on fat for the winter months ahead. But once thanks giving was over, and the harvest finished, there would be no more work until the spring, so it would be a good time to find some willing labour. Land would have to be cleared to prepare a building site, and trees would have to be cut and carted to the site. Only then could the building begin.

"So let's start planning, father," Godsbert said, rubbing his hands together excitedly. "Let's start with the site where we will build the church."

"I have two sites in mind," said Waldo, who had obviously been doing some planning already.

"So, we must be careful to choose the best one," Godsbert said.

Waldo grinned at Godsbert. "Perhaps I should have said I have two churches in mind."

"Two churches!" Godsbert exclaimed.

Waldo set down two stones a small distance apart and laid a thick pile of leaves between them.

"This stone is Seeburg ... this one is Trailfingen .... and in between them is a very dark and dangerous section of forest. I'm sure we can convince people that it is even more threatening and terrifying than it really is. Merchants and other folk must pass through it on their journeys north and south."

He paused and grinned at Godsbert: "But I think they would be extremely foolish to try and travel through that extremely fearsome piece of forest without God's help, don't you?"

"But is it so much more fearsome than other parts of the – " Godsbert cut himself short: "Yes," he said, catching on. "It is a place of evil spirits and supernatural demons. The home of the Devil himself."

"Belief is reality, Godsbert," Waldo said. "We must be persuasive."

Waldo pointed to his stones and leaves again: "If we have one church at Seeburg and one at Trailfingen, we can offer God's help to frightened travellers on both sides of the fearsome and forbidding forest."

†

With no building to be done for several weeks, Godsbert threw himself into the planning process with great energy and enthusiasm. He was much inspired by Waldo's remark, *'Belief is reality'* and proved himself to have a very inventive mind with impressive artistic skills. He had learnt the art of tree trunk carving from his father and proposed a remarkable idea to Waldo.

"We will call the forest between Seeburg and Trailfingen the *'Devil's Passage'*. I will select two large tree trunks close to the beginning of the forest path, one at Seeburg and the other one at Trailfingen. Then I will carve a large and very evil looking face of Satan into each tree trunk, four or five times larger than life size."

Godsbert made a frightening facial expression, with his hands raised like claws.

"Then," he continued vehemently, "if people want God's protection after they pass Satan's face and travel through the Devil's Passage, they must first convert to Christianity and receive a special blessing from you before they begin their journey. Perhaps the blessing involves the tree carving. You convert and bless them in the church, but they must touch the Satan face as they pass by or the blessing won't work and they will meet certain death in the forest. Without your blessing, the Devil's Passage will be a passage to hell."

Waldo stared dumbfounded at Godsbert.

"Not a bad idea, Godsbert!" he finally said. "Can you really do such carvings?"

"Yes, I am very skilled, my father taught me well."

"Then start on those carvings at once."

Godsbert was delighted with Waldo's reaction, but he wasn't finished yet.

"I have been exploring the lake shore and found one area that is almost hidden from sight, which contains countless numbers of small, round black stones that have been polished by the flowing water."

He extracted one from his tunic. "See, here is one. It reminds me of a raven's eye. Legend says that ravens can see the past and the future. They are mystical birds. They provided food for the prophet Elia, and were sent out by Noah to test the flood. Ravens are thought to be messengers between God and mankind, in a way like angels."

"Perhaps ravens can also see where the Devil is hiding in the forest," Waldo said, with a laugh.

"Exactly!" Godsbert said. "We could call these small round stones ravens' eyes and give them to people to help them avoid the devil in the forest. Once they passed safely, they drop the stone in a box that we provide."

"It's a great idea, too," Waldo said. "Keep thinking Godsbert, I'm sure you can come up with plenty more. We'll need all the help we can get to convert these pagans."

†

Once the end of harvest celebrations were finished, many people had little work to do and Waldo and Godsbert found plenty of willing hands to help prepare building sites and transport timber from the forests. Soon both Seeburg and Trailfingen were a hive of activity on two small sites as Waldo's churches slowly took shape.

He was also able to secure a patch of farmland near the river at Seeburg in sight of the church where he sowed a vegetable garden and planted herbs the way he had been taught by Othmar.

He also learnt important things about plants and nature from the locals. These pagans aren't all bad, he reminded himself. They understand the complexities of the weather and the cycle of the seasons. And who am I to find fault in their belief that 'we should give back to the earth something in return for what we take away.'

The Almighty God created the earth and we are bound to respect it.

Daily life too demands respect and makes its own rules, so the new settlers quickly learnt to expect the unexpected. The vegetable and herb garden would take time to develop so Waldo and Godsbert had to decide what food they needed and where to find it.

Only God can control the weather and when He sends extremes of hot and cold, flooding rains and wild storms, large crops can fail and small vegetable gardens can be washed away overnight. Having enough food was always at the top of the list of things to pray for.

But despite all the unavoidable problems and practicalities of everyday life, Waldo could never forget the main reason he was there in the first place. "I am a missionary priest, with God's work to do," he constantly reminded himself. Sometimes he expressed those thoughts aloud without meaning to.

On the last occasion he thought out loud, Godsbert was close by: "Building two churches in the wilds of the pagan heartland is God's work," Godsbert said.

Waldo looked startled for a moment: "Was I talking to myself again? My apologies Godsbert, but I'm concerned that we haven't converted a single heathen yet! We must start soon!"

"Then we should start with the children," Godsbert said. "They are not yet totally lost to paganism and the joy of God's word. But how do we do that? Did you learn how to attract children to our church at St. Gall?"

Waldo knew Godsbert's last remark was meant to be funny, but it gave him an idea.

"We need a big celebration here to attract people, including children. We'll have a special naming and blessing of our church and make it a festive event. We need to find a loud bell of some kind, Godsbert. If we ring that the children will come."

Godsbert looked doubtful: "Where will we get a bell from?"

"There are blacksmiths in the area," Waldo said brightly. "They will have a long piece of metal that we hang inside a triangle of tree branches and ring it with a hammer. It doesn't have to be a huge bell, just a noisy one."

A local blacksmith was found who made a small, noisy bell for the oak tree triangle.

"It works like a miracle!" Godsbert said to Waldo as they watched the people coming to investigate the strange clanging sound that was ringing out across the lake and fields. They were pleased to see many children too, most of them running ahead of the adults and laughing with glee.

"Our idea has brought the children, Godsbert," Waldo, said. "I think they have encouraged the adults to come."

It was certainly a festive occasion. Waldo welcomed everybody outside the church and announced that he was naming the church in honour of John the Baptist. He then invited everyone inside to tell them the story of the Baptist.

It was mostly Godsbert who told the story because he knew the local Swabian dialect and they could understand him clearly. But then they were astounded when Waldo began talking in Latin, a strange language they didn't understand a word of. And when he began to chant his strange words, they were completely mesmerised. Waldo had certainly learnt his missionary techniques well and they were having the desired effect. And then when he put special herbs on hot coals sending the sweet smelling smoke of incense wafting through the church, catching the sunlight streaming in through the windows, the people seemed spellbound.

At the end of the service, everyone looked delighted at what they had seen, and the children were all chattering excitedly. As a final touch, Waldo gave a piece of bread and a sip of red wine to each adult. Even though it wasn't yet consecrated it served his purpose because red wine was the drink of the nobles, not the common folk of the countryside, and they looked at Waldo with great reverence.

As the people left the church and wandered back to their farms and fields, Waldo and Godsbert agreed that their first service at their little church of Seeburg had been a huge success.

23

Devotion

Sowing the seed of Christianity in the hard soil of a pagan's heart, is one thing, but growing real plants and trees has its own challenges.

"Your hands get dirty for one thing," Waldo muttered to himself as he pushed yet another grape vine cutting into the dry soil on the sunny slope above the lake. He had brought cuttings with him from Burkheim on the upper Rhine. Grape vines flourished there - but not at Seeburg. Waldo's first crop of grapes were too sour to eat so he gave up his plans for a vineyard, leaving just a few plants for decoration.

But, once he managed the all destroying snails, he was much more successful with his vegetable and herb gardens. He enjoyed digging and turning the soil and nurturing the plants. After one afternoon of long effort in the garden, he sat back and admired his handiwork with a refreshing drink of water in the cool early evening breeze.

"What do you think of my garden, Zimple?" he asked his dog lying contently next to him, her black form almost invisible in the dim light. She didn't open her eyes but pricked up her ears at the sound of her name. Waldo reached out to pat her, silently thanking the villagers who had given her to him as a guard dog for the church.

"You'll protect us won't you, Zimple?" he said, looking at her. This time there was no response from Zimple, she was sound asleep.

Waldo continued his planting activities the next morning soon after dawn prayers. He planted a weeping willow on the riverbank, a fig tree in a sunny spot behind the church, and most important of all, he put in an oak tree near the entrance to the paradise garden in memory of his father, Richbold.

As he stood watering the oak seedling, Zimple started barking and ran off a short way towards the lake. Waldo turned to see two women making their way up the path towards him.

"Greetings, my ladies," he said.

"You are Father Waldo, the Christian missionary priest?" the older of the two women asked him.

Waldo smiled and nodded: "Yes I am."

"I am Adelinde ... and this is my sister, Hildegarde."

Waldo now saw that Hildegarde was quite young, perhaps 12 or 13. She had her head bowed and said hello shyly, without looking up.

"We are seeking refuge, Father," Adelinde said. "I am recently widowed. My husband, Count Atto and our two sons were killed fighting the Huns a few days ago on the battlefield at Planckental, just across the Danube."

"The Valley of Tears," Waldo said quietly, almost to himself. He looked at Adelinde and knew that even though she was a Swabian noble, without a husband her future and her sister's, was bleak indeed. She was wise to leave home immediately because she and Hildegarde would have become the spoils of battle for the Hun victors.

"You are both welcome here," Waldo said. "I will give you food and shelter."

He called to Godsbert, who was at the back of the church watering the fig tree, to come and meet their visitors.

†

Falling in love hadn't been in Waldo's plans, but one can never know when one's heart may be stolen, and who the thief might be. He saw the sudden appearance of Adelinde in his life as a reward from God for his devotion to his missionary work so far. Well, that was what he chose to believe anyway. As he had learned from Brother Rüdiger at Reichenau Abbey, belief is reality. Deep down inside himself, where he had pushed it out of sight, was the real truth that in the long-term, his relationship with Adelinde was doomed. As a priest, he was permitted to have a wife, but as a monk in a monastery, that was not possible. What he didn't realise was that the pain of heartbreak would arrive much sooner than he could have imagined.

But ignorance is bliss and Waldo and Adelinde became lovers. It happened naturally late one warm afternoon when Waldo and Adelinde were out in their favourite part of the forest gathering flowers for the church. For Waldo, their spontaneous lovemaking was a joyous surprise. Although he had considered the idea on many occasions since Adelinde's arrival, he had never found a way to initiate it. It certainly wasn't on his mind that afternoon in the forest picking flowers. But perhaps it was on Adelinde's mind because she had given Hildegarde a number of chores to do at the church before she and Waldo left.

They had reached a sun-drenched clearing covered by a carpet of white anemone flowers. The warm spring breeze wafting through the clearing gently caressed the anemones and filled the air with a fragrance that Waldo found intoxicating. As he stood with his eyes closed, feeling the sun on his face and breathing in the forest aromas, he felt Adelinde's hand caressing him in a way that no warm breeze could do.

When he turned to face her it occurred to him that the intoxicating fragrance he could smell wasn't coming from the flowers but from Adelinde, who was now pressed against him. Both her hands were now eagerly exploring his body and he felt a heat within him that had nothing to do with the sun. He gently undid the strings of Adelinde's dress to reveal her breasts, and kissed them tenderly. When Waldo slid her dress from her shoulders, Adelinde released a soft moan as the garment slipped from her body. At the same time she had managed to free Waldo of his robes and drew him down with her as she lay on their discarded clothing among the anemone blossoms. The setting sun was now just a golden glow in among the trees, but the ardent fire in their hearts burnt with a brilliance that illuminated their passion but blinded them to the reality of their love.

It was dark when they arrived back at the church and Adelinde was worried that Hildegarde might be concerned for them.

"I don't think you need worry about that, my love," Waldo said pointing to Hildegarde who was sound asleep on her bed. "Those chores you gave her have worn her out."

Adelinde drew a warm covering over her sister and kissed her lightly on the forehead.

Waldo had poured two cups of wine and was laying out a plate of bread and cheese.

"I'm so pleased she's asleep," Adelinde said, with

exaggerated relief. "She was looking forward to arranging the flowers."

"The flowers!" Waldo cried. "We forgot to get any! What will you tell her?"

"Nothing," Adelinde said. "She's young but she's not naïve. And besides, she'll read it on my face anyway."

"Mine too," Waldo said.

Beyond his deep love for Adelinde, Waldo admired her strength and intelligence. When she first arrived she had pretended she liked reading, but he soon realised that she was not educated at all. So he taught her to read, and to write a few words. In return she became a Christian, Waldo's most precious convert.

Such was his love and devotion for Adelinde that he decided to build a church for her and Hildegarde.

"It will be an octagon church," he told the delighted sisters. He explained the resurrection and rebirth symbolism of the octagon, just as he had explained it to Charles at the church of San Vitale in Ravenna. Adelinde and Hildegarde were greatly moved by the holy meaning of the octagon and wept tears of gratitude and devotion to the Christian God who had delivered them into the safe hands of Father Waldo of Seeburg.

Waldo was moved too, and had to pause for a time before he could continue explaining his plans.

"We will build it on the northern side of the river, right

here in the centre of Seeburg," he finally managed to say, with his arms around both women. "It will be dedicated to women and called the Chapel of the Holy Mary, in honour of both Our Lady Mary the Mother of Christ and Saint Mary Magdalene his wife."

Adelinde and Hildegarde continued to weep softly and all three went down on their knees to pray to both Maries. Then a sudden thought occurred to Waldo, which he expressed aloud.

"This may be the first church ever dedicated to women," he said.

†

News of the women's octagon church, and its symbolism of rebirth, moved Godsbert as much as it had Adelinde and Hildegarde. It also seemed to fill Godsbert with a Divine inspiration that he likened to a 'Vision of the Lord.' Several months later, Waldo told Charles, when he visited Seeburg, he believed a miracle took place in his little church.

"I remember clearly," he related to Charles, "hearing Godsbert cry out in his sleep. It was a very loud cry. Not a scream exactly ... more like a fierce yell, as a warrior might use in battle. It woke me and I instantly sat up. I looked towards Godsbert's cell and think I saw the last flash of a brilliant explosion of light inside his cell. I rushed over and looked inside, but all was dark and Godsbert was sound asleep. I heard no more cries from him that night."

"Godsbert, as I've told you, was a skilful wood sculptor and carved our two extraordinary Satan head tree trunks. Next morning, when Godsbert awoke, he found a wooden carving of the Madonna and Child on the floor by his bed, with the shavings and wood chips scattered all about. It wasn't there when he went to bed."

With a dramatic flourish, Waldo removed a large cloth covering an object beside him to reveal the Madonna and Child sculpture.

"This is it! Godsbert swore he'd never seen it before. 'I didn't carve this,' he told me, with frightened eyes. Perhaps it is related to your Vision of the Lord a few days ago, I suggested. Perhaps you carved it in your sleep. He was shaking his head and looked terrified. When we took the sculpture outside into the daylight, we could see that the carving was incomplete. The Madonna was well formed and wore a crown, but the Child was only roughly chiselled with no features on its face at all."

Charles ran his hand over the Child's featureless wooden head. "Why has Godsbert not finished it?" he asked.

"He refuses to do it," Waldo said. "He says he has only to touch it, as you are doing now, and it gives him unbearable stabbing pains throughout his body.

He sees it as a warning from God not to finish the sculpture. So it has remained as it is, and will remain that way forever."

"There is one other thing. Whenever people see it here in the church, they can't resist running their hands around the unfinished Child's head, just as you were doing. On three separate occasions now, childless women who have stroked the Child's head, have fallen pregnant within a few months.

All three swore they were barren and had been trying to conceive for many years, without success. This little, unfinished wooden sculpture is becoming very famous around here and many women visit it to stroke the Child's head. Perhaps its featureless face symbolises all children yet to be born."

24

Funeral

"Dear Waldo," Bertrada said softly, "can it really be 28 years since I held you as a baby in my arms and presented you to the Bishop of Metz for your baptism?"

Waldo and Bertrada held each other in a long, tight embrace. When they finally relaxed and released one another, they both had tears glistening on their cheeks.

"Your mother was like a mother to me," Bertrada said.

"As you are to me, dear Bertrada."

"Your godfather, my beloved Pippin, is dead and we must both devote ourselves to ensuring Charles and his brother Carloman continue what he and his father Charles Martel, have built. The future of Europe and Christendom is now in their hands."

"And the Lord God's," Waldo said.

"The Franconian Empire has no better person to seek God's support for them than you Waldo, my adopted son ... and Charles's appropriated brother."

Waldo had hurried to the Church of St. Denis in Paris for Pippin's funeral the instant he had heard of the king's imminent death. He managed to get there just in time, on the day itself, rather than a day or so earlier as he would have wished. It meant he had little opportunity to see Charles who would now be joint ruler with his much younger brother Carloman. The bad blood between the brothers was obvious for all to see, though they did their best to hide it out of respect for their father.

Waldo and Charles found a few brief minutes alone to say hello and goodbye at the same time.

"I will see you in Seeburg when I can," Charles said. "Pray for me ... and ask God to watch over Bertrada. She is your mother too ... brother."

"God go with you brother ... as I will each day in my thoughts and prayers. As you were with me on my journey from St. Gall to Seeburg."

†

Back in Seeburg, autumn was setting in and the days were growing shorter, leaving more time for telling stories around a warming fire.

"Every secret wish is a prayer," Waldo told Hildegarde, who had said there were some things her heart longed for that she could never bring herself to share with anyone.

"What do you secretly pray for, Waldo?" Hildegarde said.

"Well my dear girl," Waldo said, "every secret wish may be a prayer, but not every prayer is a secret wish. My prayers are open for all to know. First, I pray for the redemption of my soul. Second, I pray for yours and Adelinde's souls. And of course, I pray for the souls of my family and congregation. It is the reason I am a priest. As the second son, I was promised to God. My destiny was always to take on the duty to save my family's souls for entry into the Kingdom of Heaven by devoting my life to the service of the Lord our God as a member of the clergy in the Holy Christian Church."

"And who was the first son?" Adelinde asked.

Waldo's heart hardened when he thought of Ruthard, but he made an effort not to let it show in his expression.

"My older brother is called Ruthard," he said. "He is the Count of Aargau and a soldier in our King Charles's army."

"Well, I think God made the right decision sending you as the second son," Adelinde said. "He didn't want to waste you on the battlefield. You wouldn't have made a good soldier."

And Ruthard wouldn't have made a good priest, Waldo thought.

"What were your parents' names, Waldo?" Hildegarde asked.

"My mother's name was Farahild. I was only a baby

when she died and I don't remember her. My father Richbold told me that she was very beautiful, and a loving mother. My father was born in the Wetterau and became Count of Breisgau. I loved him very much, but he died when I was 13 years old, while I was in Italy with Charles and his father, King Pippin."

There was a long silence as Adelinde and Hildegarde pondered the sadness that Waldo had experienced so early in life with the tragic loss of both his parents. Waldo stood up and stretched and noisily breathed in the fresh autumn night air. It sounded like a loud sigh and both women looked up at him. He wandered a few paces then stopped and stared out across the lake to some image from the past, or perhaps the future, before returning to sit with Adelinde and Hildegarde.

"My father left me this ring," Waldo said, "which was his talisman and a prized possession."

The women had asked Waldo about the ring some time ago, but he had forgotten.

"The gemstone is a Lapis lazuli," he explained. "It is a symbol of truth and friendship."

"It is beautiful," Adelinde said, with a poignant look at Hildegarde that connected them both to the sadness Waldo was feeling about his father.

There was another extended period of silence before Adelinde finally spoke.

"Did you have a milk-mother, Waldo?"

Waldo was still scrutinising the Lapis gemstone when Adelinde's voice broke into his thoughts. He looked at her in confusion for a moment, then brightened immediately when he realised what the question was.

"Yes, I did ... we did," he said. "Charles and I shared the same milk-mother, our beloved Anneliese. She was a beautiful Swabian girl, just like you two beautiful Swabian girls. Anneliese told us wonderful stories. Our favourite was about the holy martyrs Nazarius and Celsus. We couldn't get enough of it. We pestered her constantly to tell their story over and over again. The poor girl! We loved her."

The two women seemed to have no more questions, but Waldo was suddenly in the mood to talk.

"I was christened by my uncle Chrodegang, the Bishop of Metz. And King Pippin was my godfather. Charles's mother, Bertrada, carried me to the church to present me to the Bishop." Waldo paused and considered a thought that had just occurred to him.

"You know," he said, "it was my uncle Chrodegang and the great Irish missionary Boniface who were the driving force behind the holy quest to christianise Europe. They were the first to realise that the best way to unite many different tribes of people with different cultures, languages and gods, was with a single, united faith under just one god. That way they could still have their own languages and cultures but see themselves as one people, one land. And our own dear Charles embraced their idea and became Charlemagne, God's great champion of Christianisation. Once Charles was leading the forces of Christendom, the poor pagans didn't have a chance ... they had to convert or else!"

Waldo stopped talking, virtually censuring himself. He had meant his last comment as a joke, a bit of fun at Charles's expense. But the instant he said it, he knew it was no such thing. It was a brutal and terrible truth. There was that word again, he said to himself. He looked again at his father's Lapis lazuli gemstone. Friendship and truth. He knew what the truth was, but would their friendship survive it?

Adelinde and Hildegarde were giggling at Waldo's comment about Charles converting the poor pagans and he had to forcibly restrain himself from demanding they stop. Fortunately Hildegarde asked a question that took him onto another topic entirely.

"You once told us," she said, "that you had a wonderful tutor called Othmar who was very learned about plants and herbs and could heal the sick with herbal potions and unguents. You said that you are very skilled in the secrets of healing and medications."

"As a youth," Waldo said, "I was sent as a novice monk

to a monastery on the Island of Reichenau at Lake Constance. This is where I learnt how to believe in God through faith alone, and how to care for the sick and injured. Sometimes, when a monk brother became sick, it was my duty to look after him with special drink and special food to hasten his recovery.

We treated the sick in a special building at the monastery, called a hospice. We separated them from those who were in good health so they wouldn't pass their illness on them."

Hildegarde was listening to Waldo with rapt attention and didn't hide her disappointment when he stopped.

"But tell me more Father!" she cried. "Tell me about this hospice ... could we build one ourselves to heal the sick? And plant a special herb garden. You could teach me how to make healing potions and unguents."

Hildegarde was highly excited by the prospect of a hospice while Waldo was more concerned with the practicalities of such a thing. He didn't want to dash the girl's hopes and was unsure how to respond. He looked to Adelinde for silent guidance. She nodded with a knowing smile and subtle shrug that said, Why not? It will give her something worthwhile to do.

"Very well, Hildegarde," he said. "We will discuss it tomorrow and come up with a plan. But now, even the birds have gone to sleep, and we must too."

†

Early the next morning, the moment prime prayers were said, Hildegarde reminded Waldo of his promise the night before.

"Well, dear Hildegarde," Waldo said, "even before the cock crowed this morning, I was thinking of a plan for you. I think it is possible to build a hospice and a medicinal herb garden where you could care for the sick."

Hildegarde was overjoyed and hugged Waldo.

"An important consideration," Waldo said once Hildegarde released him from her embrace, "is where your hospice should be located. I know this may sound a little macabre and upset you, Hildegarde, but it is best to face the harsh reality before undertaking a venture such as this."

Hildegarde glanced anxiously at Adelinde, who squeezed her hand and smiled reassuringly.

"Despite your best efforts in trying to heal the sick, dear, sweet Hildegarde," Waldo said gently, "many of them will not survive and will need to be buried with a holy requiem in the sight of the Almighty if he is to receive them in heaven. So there will have to be a suitable cemetery in the vicinity."

Hildegarde grimaced, but understood the simple truth of Waldo's words.

"I know of a perfect place for your hospice," Waldo

said, "not far from our church at Trailfingen, in the direction of Auingen. It is in a secret part of the forest with meadows nearby. And beyond, a short walk away, is the graveyard of Gruorn."

"I will call the hospice Reichenau," Hildegarde said, "in honor of the Abbey Reichenau where you learnt the secrets of healing, dear Waldo."

Waldo smiled at Adelinde and kissed Hildegarde tenderly on the forehead.

"You will need to have a nurse or midwife at your hospice, Hildegarde," he said. "Many illnesses and deaths are associated with childbirth."

"So, we will build the hospice, a chapel and a small house for the nurse." Hildegarde replied assuredly.

†

"We write already the year 770 Anno Domini," Waldo said to Godsbert. "We have been here in Seeburg for six years. And we have achieved many things. Thank you Godsbert. God must be very proud of you, as I am."

"Holy father, you have been an inspiration to me since the day we left Reichenau," Godsbert replied. "I am blessed to have been chosen by you, and the Lord."

Waldo's sense of achievement lifted his spirits temporarily, but a heaviness in his heart continued to weigh him down. When Adelinde came up and embraced him, it took an extraordinary force of will for him not to break down with grief and sadness.

He had a foreboding that the three loves in his life were about to do battle. Already he knew in his heart that his love of God and love for Charles would leave no room for his love for Adelinde. What he didn't know was that the reason for his foreboding was already on the horizon and heading his way.

"Our love is powerful and beautiful," Waldo said. Happy in his embrace, Adelinde simply murmured her agreement.

"But our love of God is eternal and unassailable," he whispered into her sweet smelling hair, kissing her on the cheek.

And to himself he said: My love for Charles and his Christian mission is also powerful ... and unassailable.

†

Bertrada's love for both her sons consumed her every waking moment. For the two years since Pippin's death, each day of her life had been spent trying to end the feud between Charles and Carloman, now joint rulers of the Carolingian empire. Charles was the first born, but an illegitimate child. Carloman was born in wedlock and considered himself the rightful sole ruler. They hated each other and made no secret of the fact that they wanted their sibling dead. An all out war between the two brothers seemed inevitable. Their desperate mother was prepared to try anything to reconcile her two sons. Both sons adored her and she had a powerful influence over them, so they were at least prepared to listen to her.

She convinced them to agree to her latest plan that they should both marry daughters of the Lombardian king, Desiderius. It would form close ties with the powerful kingdom south of the Alps, she told them, and provide a staunch ally for future conflicts. What she didn't tell them was that she hoped that marrying sisters might bring them closer together and help heal the ill will between them.

The two brothers married the Lombardian princesses and Bertrada's bold plan seemed to be working. But not long after, her hopes were dashed once more when Charles changed his mind and wanted to leave his Lombardian wife Desiderada and return to his concubine Hilmitrude with whom he had two illegitimate children already.

As a last resort, Bertrada travelled to Liège and spent Easter there with Charles.

"Carloman has taken to calling me 'The Bastard Pretender' in public, at every opportunity," a furious Charles told his mother. "It must stop … now!" he bellowed, crashing both his fists down on the table they were dining at, jolting plates and toppling wine goblets.

Bertrada saw the seething hatred in Charles's eyes and despaired for both her sons.

After Easter she left Charles at Liège with the heaviest heart she had felt since Pippin's death. She made for Carloman's stronghold at Seltz on the river Rhine.

Carloman refused to cease his push for sole, legitimate rule and refrain from calling Charles 'The Bastard Pretender'.

But he knew that in a war with his brother, Charles's superior forces would prevail.

"If we find a strong ally for you," Bertrada said, "it will even up the contest and Charles may think twice about fighting you." Carloman was still happily married to his Lombardian wife and was now the brother-in-law of Tassilo III the Duke of Bavaria, who was also married to a daughter of the Lombardian King Desiderius.

"Tassilo may be prepared to help me," Carloman said. "He will probably need my help in Bavaria in the future fighting the Slavs."

"I will travel to Passau and see Tassilo," Bertrada said. "The weather is improving, so I will leave very soon."

Seeburg, May 15, 770AD

25

Mission

Bertrada was used to travelling with Pippin, who had never established a permanent imperial residence. He was constantly on the move with his army to battlefields all over his empire, and beyond. Bertrada had learnt to travel with him, and like all nobles, took her servants and household with her.

She knew travelling across country in those parts would be a challenge because established roads were non-existent. Those that did exist were badly deteriorated and falling apart, ancient roads left behind by the Romans two hundred years earlier. The most convenient route for Bertrada to take on her journey to Passau was over the Swabian Alb along river beds until she reached the river Neckar. From there she could travel along the river Erms until she arrived at the shallowest crossing to take her over the Alb and down to the Danube, on which she could travel in some comfort, by boat, to Passau.

Her route from Seltz to Passau along the Erms took her through Seeburg in mid May 770 AD.

"Dear Waldo," Bertrada said, "we meet again. Two

more years have passed and the pain in my heart is worse than on the day Pippin died."

"Charles and Carloman are still at each other's throats?" Waldo said, trying not to sound too concerned. His tone had a casual air about it, as if he was saying 'boys will be boys.'

But Bertrada was having none of it, and her eyes flared. "They are determined to kill one another!" she cried. "They are on the verge of outright war! I can't bear it, Waldo." Waldo's name trailed off like a moan and she began sobbing on his shoulder.

As he held her close and stroked her head, Waldo knew that the brothers' feud would never end and only the abdication by one of them would resolve it. Beyond that, only the death of Charles or Carloman would bring harmony to the Carolingian dynasty.

Waldo had always been awed by Bertrada's mental strength and resilience. He felt her stop sobbing and push away from him. She stood wiping her eyes for several seconds and then was back in control of her emotions.

"I am travelling to Passau to ask Tassilo to support Carloman," she said. "Perhaps if Carloman has a strong ally, Charles won't attack him. It is my last hope, Waldo. Yet, he seems set on a war with his brother."

Bertrada stopped herself and closed her eyes. She seemed to be listening to sounds outside the church, or deep inside her own head. Waldo knew what she was thinking.

"If only we had waited, Pippin and I, ... waited to be married ... my sons would not be trying to kill each other."

It seemed she would begin sobbing again, but she visibly steeled herself and found something to distract her.

"I have brought you a present, dearest Waldo."

She reached into a leather satchel and withdrew a book written on fine goatskin.

"It is a book of neums, music notation," she said.

Waldo was thunderstruck. He couldn't believe his ears ... or his eyes. He was lost for words, so Bertrada continued talking.

"They are used to indicate patterns of rhythm called rhythmic nodes and are a wonderful help in performing Gregorian chanting."

Waldo was nodding rapidly, Yes! Yes! ... he was trying to get the words out.

"Astonishing!" he finally blurted out. "I can't believe it! Neums were first discovered in ancient literature at the monastery of Metz, where my uncle was the bishop. The same bishop you handed me over to at my christening Bertrada!"

He hugged her with great joy, overcome with gratitude. "It is the most wonderful gift you could have given me Bertrada."

She drew away, smiled broadly at him, and kissed him on both cheeks.

"I'm so happy you like it, Waldo," she said, very sweetly. And then grasped him firmly by both shoulders. "You may have to earn it," she said. "I will need your help with Charles and Carloman. Seeburg may have to do without you."

26

Visit

"You missed her by two days, Charles," Waldo said. "She has gone over the Alb, to Passau."

A clearly frustrated Charles paced in a circle around the room for almost a minute without speaking. He then stopped and punched his fist into his hand: "I have been following that woman since she crossed the Rhine."

He stared hard at Waldo: "Passau, you say? She's going to Passau?"

Charles began pacing again, and then finally sat down. He leant forward, hands on his thighs, and glowered at Waldo, who had sat down opposite him.

"Now why is my mother going to Passau?" Charles asked aggressively, as if somehow Waldo was responsible for Bertrada's movements.

"I'm on your side, Charles," Waldo said calmly. "You know why she's going to Passau."

Charles waved one hand in a gesture of apology.

"Tassilo won't be any use to Carloman," he said. "It won't matter who he gets on his side, I'll crush him anyway!"

Waldo saw no point in discussing Charles and

Carloman's feud. If Charles had wanted his advice on it, he would have asked, and he hadn't. And besides, he and Charles knew what had to be done. Finding a way to rid Charles of his rebellious brother without destroying Bertrada in the process, was the unspoken but indisputable understanding between the two men.

Charles stood up.

"This summer heat is intolerable. Let's walk together and find some shade and a cooling breeze," he said.

They walked along the path that led to the trail through the forest to Trailfingen.

"Our Satan's head," Waldo said, stopping at Godsbert's tree trunk carving.

Charles laughed heartily, but he was impressed with Godsbert's workmanship.

"We'll continue walking," he said. "I don't want the Devil overhearing what I'm about to say." Another hearty laugh. He then became thoughtful and serious: "You already know that I trust you more than anyone in the world, Waldo. I can talk to my advisers and generals about most things, but not everything. I need a personal adviser ... and a confessor. Someone who can accept and forgive the unavoidable sins I must commit as a king and defender of Christianity. You alone can fill that role, Waldo."

"In Persona Christi," Waldo said.

"Yes," Charles responded quickly. "In the person of

Christ."

He stopped walking. Waldo continued a few paces on before stopping himself. He stared out over the beautiful lake and landscape beyond. He turned his head and his gaze fell on his beautiful little church nestled among trees near the river. He knew what was coming and felt a tightness in his chest.

Charles caught up to him and stood at his side. He didn't look at Waldo but fixed his gaze on the church as well.

"Unfortunately," he said, "you cannot be my Persona Christi stuck here at a little church in remote Seeburg. You must go and be a monk at St. Gall."

Waldo nodded his acceptance of Charles's wishes, but said nothing.

"I cannot achieve my destiny without you behind me, my brother Waldo. It is *our* destiny."

I hope I am up to our joint destiny, Waldo thought.

The two men momentarily made eye contact before returning their attention to some distant points across the lake. Occasionally when he looked directly into Charles's eyes, fleeting visions of future events flashed through his mind. He had heard it said that the eyes are windows to the soul, but for Waldo, his friend's illuminated eyes sometimes reflected events Charles's soul had yet to experience ... and justify. Such fleeting visions had once occurred between the two when they were boys, and neither Waldo nor Charles had forgotten it.

Waldo's prolonged silence began to concern Charles. He turned and looked at his friend.

"Are you seeing our destiny now, Waldo?"

"What I am seeing is a future flowing with the blood of unbelievers. I don't think it's a future God wants me to contribute to."

"God will make that decision, not you, not I," Charles said. "Our destiny can be nothing except what God wills it to be. It is out of our hands. Our job is to build and defend Christendom, whatever it takes. He will let us know if we take it too far."

Charles threw both his arms wide and smiled. "The past is unchangeable, the future is unknowable, all we have is now. So let us embrace what we have today – our great love and friendship, and an exciting life ahead together doing God's work. Tonight we shall have a feast to celebrate your move to St. Gall, the next step in your destiny!"

Charles's exuberance, if not his words, seemed to cheer Waldo up. He managed a smile and the two men firmly clasped each other's arms.

"So," Charles said, "what's in the larder for us to feast on?"

"Carrots, beans and a marrow," Waldo said. "And some

wine."

"Good, good," Charles said. "But we also need roast meat! I will take some men into the forest and bring back a boar or deer before nightfall."

†

The sun was low in the sky when Charles and his men returned from the hunt, but the air was still hot from a long day of high temperatures. The horses were lathered in sweat, their heads hanging low with exhaustion. Their riders too were spent and dragged themselves wearily from their saddles.

"A successful hunt!" Charles announced between great gulps of water from a pitcher that Godsbert handed to him the instant he dismounted. "We killed a plump young boar for our feast tonight."

"We anticipated your triumphant return," Waldo said. "Godsbert has set up a roasting spit and fire beside our little octagon church of the Holy Mother Mary. We will give thanks to her for providing this wonderful meat from the forest ... and then we will roast it to perfection!"

Several hours later, the feasting over, Charles's exhausted men quickly fell asleep on the ground well away from the fire. Only one soldier didn't sleep. It was his job to take the first shift as a sentry watching over Charles. Godsbert, Adelinde and Hildegarde had already retired to their beds. Charles and Waldo remained awake, sitting opposite one another. Waldo was lying back with his legs stretched out on a large timber bench seat Godsbert had carved from a fallen tree trunk. King Charles had taken his rightful place on a crudely made throne-shaped seat that Godsbert had fashioned from wood and iron hinges. Charles had been greatly amused by the rough wooden throne when he first arrived, but he had found it most comfortable and used it at every opportunity, much to its maker's delight.

As the two men sat talking quietly, Charles began to tremble, but it ceased after several seconds. Waldo, who had been lying back admiring the starlit sky, heard the brief tremble in Charles's voice. He sat up and looked at his friend.

Seeing Waldo's reaction, Charles waved a dismissive hand at him. "It's nothing," he said, "just lack of proper sleep of late from agitation caused by my mother's interference in my marital affairs. I do not want to be married to that dull Lombardian princess – but Bertrada is determined to persuade me. I cannot bear the thought of being without my beloved sweetheart Hilmitrude and our children. I will retire now with her in my mind. Perhaps thoughts of her kisses and caresses will help me sleep."

As he stood up to go, he began to tremble again. This time it didn't pass quickly and in less than a minute he was trembling violently. Charles's sentry rushed over to see him collapse on the ground, still trembling. He bent down to assist his king, but Waldo stopped him with a sharp command.

"Stop! Don't restrain him, let it pass."

As the bewildered soldier stood up and stepped back, Charles's seizure began to subside.

A look of fear replaced the confusion on the soldier's face. "Is the king possessed by the devil?" he asked, wide-eyed.

"No, he is not possessed," Waldo said calmly. "It is just the temporary effect of the heat and exhaustion of today's hunt. As well as many nights lack of sleep due to the many problems a great king must confront to allow the rest of us to sleep restfully in our beds."

Waldo gestured towards the other soldiers.

"Please go and wake your companions," he said, "and stir Godsbert and the women from their beds."

Soon after, the soldiers carried the unconscious Charles into the small octagon church and laid him on comfortable bedding that Adelinde and Hildegarde quickly set up.

Waldo's medical training ensured that everything

possible was done for Charles in the circumstances. He instructed Adelinde and Hildegarde to take turns staying with Charles throughout the night.

"Apart from the seizure," Waldo said, "Charles also has a fever, so you will have to try and keep his head cool with wet cloths."

"I will look after him for the first few hours," Adelinde said, "and then Hildegarde can take over till morning."

While the two women attended to Charles, Waldo took Godsbert aside.

"Charles's seizure was not a result of heat exhaustion and prolonged lack of sleep, as I told the soldier," he said. "Nor was he possessed by the Devil. We were taught about this affliction at St. Gall. It is a mysterious disorder that comes and goes."

"What is it called?" Godsbert asked, with a touch of fear in his voice.

"It has no agreed name," Waldo said. "The Greek physician Hippocrates called it the Sacred Disease. He refuted the idea that it is a curse or the result of some diabolical power and proved it was a disease."

Waldo paused and thought for a moment. "Perhaps it should be called epilepsia, which is from the Greek word for seizure," he mused. "I'm surprised Hippocrates didn't think of that."

"It is a terrifying disease whatever it's called," Godsbert

said, frowning and shaking his head.

"There is no cure or treatment," Waldo explained. "Only Jesus Himself was able to cure it. In the Gospel according to Mark, Jesus Christ cast out a devil from a young man with this affliction whose father had brought the boy to Him. 'Teacher,' he said, 'This is my son, who is possessed by a demon that has robbed him of speech. Whenever it seizes him, it throws him to the ground. He trembles uncontrollably, gnashes his teeth, and becomes rigid. I asked your disciples to drive the evil spirit out, but they could not.'"

"But Jesus could?" Godsbert said.

"He could ... and did," Waldo said. Then he sighed. "Unfortunately the Lord didn't see fit to pass on the technique."

Godsbert looked at Waldo strangely, almost reproachfully.

"Yes Godsbert, I know, that was an irreverent remark. But we do not have the Lord's power to work miracles. I just wish He would give us some clues about curing the terrible diseases and afflictions so many people have to suffer. I suppose if He has chosen to curse Charles the Great King, His own greatest Christian soldier and champion of Christendom with epilepsia, then those of us humble folk who are unfortunate enough to get the disease will have to learn to live with it."

"Or die with it," Godsbert said sadly.

"Ah well, my dear Godsbert," Waldo said, "that is ultimately why we are here, to die ... and hopefully join the Lord in heaven when we do."

†

Charles didn't die during the night, but he tossed and turned relentlessly, often crying out in his delirium. With the constant nursing throughout, firstly by Adelinde and then Hildegarde, the stricken king lived to see the sunrise. In his confusion, the rays of the sun at first seemed like a divine light from heaven and he initially thought he had joined the angels. Was there not one looking at him when he first opened his eyes? The first face he saw when he awoke was Hildegarde's and he was convinced she was an angel sent by the Virgin Mary to escort him to heaven.

"You are my Guardian Angel!" Charles cried out shielding his eyes from the glare of the sunlight now filling the small room.

"No, my king, I am Hildegarde."

Charles grasped Hildegarde's hand and attempted to sit up, but he immediately slumped back down with a loud groan, still gripping her hand. To Hildegarde it seemed that he had fainted. With her free hand she once again began applying the cool, damp cloth to Charles's forehead.

A short time later she tried to extricate her hand from his firm grip. As she did so, Charles opened his eyes.

"So, I am not dead," he said, with a weak smile, "and this is not heaven. But you are still an angel. The Lord has sent you to save me. He still has work for me to do."

Charles touched the damp cloth that Hildegarde was holding against his forehead when he opened his eyes. She had instantly withdrawn it, as if she thought she might be breaking some law by laying a hand on the king.

"How long have you been attending to my fever with this cloth?" Charles asked.

"Most of the night, my lord."

"Then we have spent our first night together," he said with a croaky laugh, again trying to sit up, before slumping back down again. This time he had fainted, or instantly fallen asleep, still holding Hildegarde's hand. She looked at her hand in his but made no attempt to extricate it. The long vigil at Charles's bedside had exhausted her and she laid her head down on the edge of the bed. Seconds later she was sound asleep.

During the next few days of Charles's recuperation, Hildegarde was by his side. Charles's head was still full of divine dreams and macabre nightmares induced by his seizure and fever.

"In one dream," he said, "a man appeared before me saying he had a gift for me from God. It was a golden long sword, as high as your fair head, dear Hildegarde. The sword signifies the power of the Carolingian dominion. On its blade were written four words. Near the hilt was the word raht, then radoleiba, and nasg, and near the point of the sword was the word enti. Raht means abundance of all things. Radoleiba means a rapid decline in everything. Nasg says the rulers will raise taxes for sordid profit and exploit the people. And enti means end. Either the end of the world, or the end of our dynasty."

Hildegarde was listening closely, but said nothing.

"I am not a believer in omens," Charles said, "but the dream is a reminder that we are beginning to enjoy the abundance that my grandfather and my father fought so long and hard for. It tells me that I cannot allow the decline to occur, or let my nobles and clergy exploit the people with taxes and greed. The end will come ultimately, when God wills it."

He paused and tenderly stroked Hildegarde's head.

"I will make a gold long sword – the height of your fair head, my angel – but there will be only two words engraved on it, raht and enti."

He withdrew his hand as he struggled to control a fervour that burned brightly in his eyes.

"There will be no radoleiba and nasg while I am alive!" he boomed, slamming an open hand down on a small table beside his bed, dislodging a bowl of fruit.

Hildegarde jumped with fright and immediately bent down to retrieve the bowl and fruit. As she did so, Charles saw the back of her head and noticed for the first time how beautifully her hair was arranged. Her long locks were intricately plaited like golden rope, then drawn back and gathered in two large loops that rested on her neck and shoulders. The plaits were entwined with glittering gold and silver braid, which was tied in a bow that held the looped plaits in place.

As Hildegarde placed the bowl of fruit back on the table, Charles reached out and gently ran the back of his hand down her cheek. He picked up a rosy, brightly polished apple from the bowl and studied it.

"Love is a fruit in season at all times," he said, "and within the reach of every hand."

Hildegarde blushed the colour of the apple. But she surprised Charles with her reply for one so young and innocent.

"Love is, above all, the gift of oneself," she murmured softly.

"Will you give me the gift of your love, Hildegarde?" he said.

"Yes, my lord ... once you are well enough."

"The promise of your love is a powerful medicine."

"It is the healing power of the Virgin Mary that has cured you, my lord. I prayed to the Holy Mother through the night, here in Mary's Chapel, named after her."

"Then I will make a promise to you, dear Hildegarde," Charles said. "I will one day build an octagon church of stone in honour of the Virgin Holy Mother. In this church I will go down on my knees and thank her for releasing one of her angels from heaven and sending her to look after me in my hour of need."

†

Several days later, Ruthard's childhood friend Warin, now Count Warin of Thurgau arrived at Seeburg to vow his support for Charles in his feud with Carloman. Waldo had still not forgiven Warin for his conspiracy with Ruthard and the Bishop of Constance to banish Othmar to Werd Island where he starved to death. But he had to respect Warin's loyalty to Charles and he was able, with God's help, to control his anger and disgust.

The three men spent many hours plotting against Carloman, although only in the aspects of warfare. Charles and Waldo's oath to have Carloman secretly killed was not shared with Warin, or anyone else. It would be their deed, and sin, alone.

Whenever the women were present, the men put aside their talk of war and discussed Waldo's holy work as a missionary. But when military men speak of religion, it still sounds like war.

"But who's side is God on," Adelinde asked, "when two Christian armies do battle?"

"When both sides in a battle pray to God for victory," Warin answered, "it puts the Lord in an impossible situation. So his only recourse is to be scrupulously fair and not to assist either side and let the best army win. Of course the winning army assumes God was on their side."

"God is on the side of those with the best weapons, tactics and soldiers," Charles said.

"Can you never find it in your hearts to forgive your enemies?" Adelinde said.

"Forgiving them is God's role," Warin said. "Our job is simply to arrange the meeting."

Warin's arrival had taken Waldo's mind back to his childhood and family at Breisgau. Now it was going back even further, to his own christening, not that he remembered it, of course. But he knew it was when Bertrada and Pippin created Charles.

His godmother Duchess Williswinda had died recently and he was saddened that he could not attend her funeral.

Waldo wasn't to know, but if the Duchess was with them now at Seeburg, she would be smiling broadly at Charles's fascination with Adelinde's younger sister,

Hildegarde. Just as she was smiling at his father Pippin's enthralment with Bertrada at Waldo's christening. If I was there Waldo, she would say, I would have great fun teasing Charles, just as I teased his father.

Like Duchess Williswinda, Adelinde was a keen observer of human behaviour. She saw clearly that Charles was captivated with Hildegarde, although Charles imagined he was hiding it well enough.

Adelinde brought it to Waldo's attention.

"Are you sure?" he asked, mildly shocked. "I hadn't noticed."

"Of course you hadn't," Adelinde said.

A day or so later, Waldo had to admit that Adelinde was right.

"Charles's besotted with Hildegarde," he said.

Waldo didn't tell Adelinde about all the complications and problems he saw ahead in Charles's desire for Hildegarde. Adelinde was deeply protective of her younger sister and only wanted what was best for her. A Carolingian king was a most acceptable suitor for Hildegarde as far as she was concerned. A few complications and problems would be a small price to pay.

Charles realised soon enough that he was fooling nobody and one night, as they were all eating, he declared his deep love for Hildegarde. Adelinde had warned her sister it would happen, so Hildegarde was well prepared. And very happy, because she had fallen for Charles too.

"This will be no forced marriage," Charles said to Waldo later that evening. "But it will be a delayed one. Once I have dealt with Carloman, I will divorce Desiderata and marry Hildegarde. Such a delay is also necessary because Hildegarde is very young."

Yes she is, Waldo thought, she is just 13! But he didn't express his thought aloud.

"She is a virgin, Waldo," Charles said, "and I want her to remain so until I return to marry her. In the meantime, you must keep her safe for me. You must ensure that her innocence and purity is protected, Waldo. I cannot marry her if she has lain with another man."

Waldo had another thought that he wasn't prepared to say out loud. Hildegarde may have her own thoughts about the timing and circumstances of the loss of her virginity, he told himself.

Charles's besotted attention and declaration of love may have awakened feelings in Hildegarde's mind and body that she didn't know existed before. She may not be able to 'keep her knees together' as Charles had crudely put it, if she didn't see him for many months.

She was a beautiful young woman and would surely inflame the passions of most young men she met. He even had his suspicions about Godsbert's intentions towards Hildegarde because he had noticed him on many occasions regarding her with a wistful and faraway look in his eyes.

The girl may decide his novice assistant would be a pleasant distraction until Charles returned.

"I do not expect you to be able to watch over her purity every moment of the day and night, Waldo," Charles said. "But perhaps you can give her a 'spiritual' protection, a sense of her responsibility to retain her virginity in the eyes of God, now that she is betrothed to the king."

"Are you betrothed?"

"Not officially," Charles said, slightly irritated by Waldo's question. "I have not made any promises, of course. But I have expressed my love for her. If it continues, I will marry her when I think the time is right. So press upon her, Waldo, that her pure young body is a sacred vessel until I return. Keep her safe ... by whatever means is required."

Waldo doubted his ability to keep her safe even while he was in Seeburg, but as a monk in a monastery, it would be impossible. And with what he had seen, he could hardly ask Godsbert to be her protector.

Beyond Charles's personal concerns, he was also still coping with the torment in his own heart at the prospect of leaving Adelinde. Both of them had come to terms with the fact that they would have to part. Adelinde was now a devout Christian and she saw Waldo's new life in a monastery as devotion to the love of God. It was their own deep love for one another that God was taking in return.

"I want to keep Adelinde safe too," he said to Charles. "For her sake, not mine. I will be a monk in a monastery. She will be an unmarried woman at the mercy of all manner of brute and scoundrel."

"Between us we will keep them both safe," Charles said. "I have a plan."

Waldo looked relieved at Charles's assurance. Then his face was overcome with an expression of pure mischief.

"It's amazing how much Hildegarde reminds me of our beloved milk-mother, Anneliese," he said. "She even speaks the same Swabian dialect and has a similar hairstyle."

"I hadn't noticed," Charles said as he turned and walked off, leaving Waldo grinning like an idiot.

27

Donation

Thank God there are so many pagans in the world, Waldo said to himself. And Christian sinners too. Where would the Church be without sinners and heathens? We'd all be out of a job.

He had been listening to a rather naive question from the young Hildegarde.

"What happens," she asked, "when you have converted everyone to Christianity? Will you close all the churches and monasteries? There would be no more need for them."

Waldo smiled at her, and replied warmly, being careful not to sound patronising.

"I pray constantly that our services will one day be unnecessary," he said, feeling less than honest.

Hildegarde's next question was not so naive.
"Why must we convert the pagans?"

Waldo was still considering an answer when Godsbert jumped in first.

"The pagans don't know they are sinning against God," he said. "But we must tell them. We can't have them thinking they are on earth to enjoy themselves. They are here as a punishment, like the rest of us Christians are. Why should the pagans not also feel the terrible wrath of God?"

Waldo looked at Godsbert in astonishment. I don't think Brother Rüdiger would be too impressed with that kind of straight-talking, he thought. But Godsbert seemed very pleased with himself, and Hildegarde was nodding, apparently happy with the answer.

Waldo made a mental note to discuss basic missionary psychology with Godsbert at a later date.

At that moment Charles walked in.

"Waldo!" he announced. "You are leaving Seeburg soon. So we must immediately consider the matter of donating your churches."

"I have been giving it some thought," Waldo replied. "Godsbert has written it down for me."

Godsbert disappeared briefly, before returning with a tattered piece of vellum.

"Please read it out, Godsbert," Waldo said.

Godsbert cleared his throat: "I am in God's name Waldo and donate a gift, as documented, for the wellbeing of my soul, donated to the holy martyr Nazarius, whose body rests in Cloister Lorsch, where the abbot Gundeland is responsible in the name of Rome, that I shall always be present in the Alemannic area of

Muensingen and Auingen, a church, farmland and meadows and also a church in the village of Trailfingen and another one in Seeburg. Documented in Cloister Lorsch on June 11 in the second year of reign by King Carolus, consecrated in his presence."

"Take out the last four words, consecrated in his presence," Charles said.

"You promised you would be there for the consecration," Waldo said.

"If I am upright and breathing when the time comes, I will be there. But that will be for the Lord God to decide, not me. Take it out."

Waldo nodded at Godsbert, who nodded back.

"It's out."

"Now that is done," Charles said cheerily, "Waldo and I need to speak privately."

As the others left the room, Charles and Waldo sat at a table next to each other. Charles had unfurled a roughly drawn map.

"This is how we will keep Hildegarde and Adelinde safe," he said, placing his forefinger on the map. "Here is Lake Federsee, between Seeburg and St. Gall. We will build a refuge there, a nunnery – a monastery for women. Construction can begin soon, while there is plenty of summer left."

"Who will pay for this building?" Waldo said.

"Ah well," Charles said, "Warin is a loyal supporter of mine now and has offered to fund the monastery."

"That is a lot of loyalty," Waldo said. "It will be costly, a building on the lake."

"He had a little additional incentive to spur on his sense of charity and good will," Charles said, smiling broadly.

"You and I have an old score to settle with Warin. I told him that if he builds the women's monastery, the score is settled. His part in Othmar's death will be forgiven and forgotten. But you also have to agree that the score is settled."

Waldo rationalised his decision by convincing himself that Othmar would also forgive and forget for the sake of the two women.

"I agree," he said, looking Charles square in the eye.

†

"The month of June," Waldo said to Godsbert, "in this the year of 770 Anno Domini, will be a very busy one." He paused, choosing his words carefully. "And it will be both a sad and joyous one."

It was decided that Godsbert should stay and take charge of the churches at Seeburg and Trailfingen. After six years missionary training with Waldo, Godsbert was soon to be ordained a priest. He considered the role of running the churches a great honour and privilege, but he wondered if the parting of ways with Waldo was too big a price to pay.

"As the great Boniface said, as missionaries we are soldiers of Christ," Waldo said. "We march into battle wherever He needs us. He needs you here, and me at St. Gall. We will always be comrades-at-arms in the Lord's army, you and I Godsbert. Distance can never separate our hearts and souls from one another."

"God bless you, father," Godsbert said. "I will not fail you here in Seeburg."

"That's the spirit, Godsbert! Now, there is much to do."

"Starting with donating the churches to the Cloister Lorsch," Godsbert said.

"Everything must be in place for June 11, so I will begin making the final arrangements."

"Don't forget to note somewhere that Charles has promised to visit the Cloister Lorsch in due course so he can be present when the monestary's church is consecrated in the name of the holy martyr, Nazarius. I'll get Charles to put his seal on the note so he can't change his mind."

"When will you leave?" Godsbert asked, finding something to look at other than Waldo's face.

"A week or so after the donations are complete."

Godsbert seemed to want to say something, but was having trouble getting the words out.

"Speak up, Godsbert," Waldo said, "what's on your mind?"

"Thank you father," Godsbert said. "I have in mind to make a sculpture garden here near the octagon church. Would you permit me to do that?"

"I can't see why not, Godsbert. Why would I object?"

"I thought a garden filled with carvings and statues may seem too pagan to you, as if it appeared people were worshipping false or unholy images."

"But there would be some sculptures of saints and the holy Mother of God?"

"Of course," Godsbert said.

"Well then ..." Waldo said with a wave of his hand.

"Our first sculpture," Godsbert said," is the Virgin Mary holding the faceless child." He paused as his brow creased into a deep scowl.

"That was nothing to be afraid of, Godsbert," Waldo said kindly. "It was simply the Lord reminding you of your great talent as a wood carver."

Godsbert's face brightened. "Perhaps you're right, master," Godsbert said. "My garden will be a paradise garden. A Garden of Eden ... with sculptures."

"I'm sure if Adam and Eve had your wood carving skills, Godsbert, there would have been sculptures in the Garden of Eden. Show me where you will build this garden."

Godsbert was overjoyed with Waldo's response to his

idea and chatted excitedly as the two men made their way to the northern bank of the river to the little octagon church they had built for Adelinde and Hildegarde.

"It will spread out from here," he said, extending both arms in a wide, sweeping motion.

"If this town continues to grow as it seems to be doing, Godsbert," Waldo said looking around in every direction, "your garden will be right in the centre of town."

"Perfect!" Godsbert said. "Seeburg can blossom around our garden. Let me take you on a guided walk through the future Paradise Garden of Seeburg."

He strode forward and paced out three locations.

"It will have three lakes of different sizes," he said as he stopped pacing. "One here, one over there and another, the smallest one, behind us over there. There will also be a bridge just there. Let's walk to the bridge."

He stopped again after about 20 strides.

"We are standing where the start of the bridge will be," he said. "I will make more tree stump carvings ... maybe even one in your likeness, Father Waldo, so you will be here with us forever! A full length, life size image of you carved in wood with your feet firmly rooted in the sacred soil of Seeburg!"

"I think a likeness of a saint would be more appropriate, Godsbert," Waldo said sternly, but smiling inside at Godsbert's affection and loyalty. "Perhaps a small altar would be an appropriate addition to your garden."

"An excellent suggestion, Father!" Godsbert declared. "I will also cut the legs off a wooden bench and place it on the river's edge so weary travellers can dangle their feet in the cool water on a hot day."

"Ingenious!" Waldo said. "But with clever ideas like that, Godsbert, be prepared for the locals to make fun of you." Godsbert waved his hand dismissively. "They won't laugh once they try it. And of course there will be all those other things that are required of a paradise garden ... lots of vegetables, plants and flowers."

"It is a wonderful plan, Godsbert. It has my blessing. Let us kneel here on the bridge and ask the Lord God to make your paradise garden lush and fruitful."

"Generous Father, who satisfies the hunger of all creatures, we praise you for making the earth fruitful so that it might produce what is needed for life. Oh Risen Christ you revealed yourself to us as one who provides for the poor and cares for all people. Bless those who work in the fields and give us seasonable weather. Almighty God grant that Godsbert will find some samaritan helpers so his paradise garden at Seeburg will be lush and fruitful and that all who enter it will rejoice in Your goodness. This we ask in the name of our Lord Jesus Christ. Amen."

Godsbert hunched over and kissed the earth. He remained like that for several minutes weeping with joy and the pure love of God.

"Come, Godsbert," Waldo finally said, gently helping the novice to his feet.

"Thank you Father, for the beautiful prayer."

"The good Lord was listening and will heed our prayer," Waldo said. "I'm sure your garden will endure many years, and people will see it and remember Godsbert of Seeburg, master sculptor and gardener!"

"And if over time the garden is forgotten and overgrown with weeds, all will not be lost!" Godsbert declared with great hope and humour. "A special man of passion and vision in the distant future will recreate my garden right here on this spot. He will do it as a tribute to the memory of the wonderful Father Waldo and his humble assistant Godsbert, who converted the pagans of Seeburg and its surroundings the gentle way, with love and holy devotion to the cross, not with hate and brutal allegiance to the sword."

"Well said, Godsbert!" Waldo exclaimed. "I'm sure the Lord will find such a man. Now, come with me, I have something for your garden."

Waldo led Godsbert back to the south side of the river and into the church. He leant behind the altar and took out a narrow wooden box of a size that would accommodate a large dinner plate. He placed the box on the altar and then extracted a small item from the folds of his robe. Godsbert immediately recognised it as the small wooden sundial Waldo carried everywhere with him.

"You have always admired my timepiece," Waldo said. "Some time ago when I was looking at it, I thought of an idea for a parting gift for you."

He handed the box to Godsbert.

"Of course, at the time I didn't know about your plans for a garden - perhaps the good Lord put the idea in my head – because it will be a most suitable addition."

When Godsbert saw what was in the box he was overjoyed for the second time that afternoon, but he resisted a repeat of his tearful response earlier.

"It is magnificent!" he cried.

"It is an iron replica of my tiny sundial," Waldo said happily. "Much larger as you can see, and quite heavy. The skilled blacksmith who made our church bell did it for me. He has included several holes so that you can fix it to the top of a post."

"Thank you Father! Thank you!" Godsbert exclaimed. "I will go and find a suitable post immediately."

Waldo held out a restraining arm: "Have you forgotten, Godsbert? My timepiece tells me we are due to say nones prayers. There will be time for your sundial later," he said, emphasising the word time and grinning at Godsbert.

Godsbert looked blank momentarily, but quickly

picked up Waldo's joke and laughed appreciatively. "Most humorous, Father," he said.

After nones, as Godsbert hurried off to find a post for his sundial, Waldo saw Charles striding towards him.

"My messengers have found Bertrada," Charles said. "She is on her way back from Passau and will be coming through Seeburg in a few days. I will wait for her here."

"Give her my greetings, Charles," Waldo said. "And tell her I say a special prayer for her every day."

"And what would that special prayer be for, I wonder?" Charles said with an exaggerated glare at Waldo.

"That is between your mother and her favourite priest. In Persona Christi."

"Let's hope that special prayer doesn't work, Waldo," Charles said. "I don't actually say it. I just want your mother to think I do," Waldo replied.

The two men embraced briefly, but powerfully, the bond since childhood even stronger than ever. The cross and the sword. The sword and the cross.

"I will see you at St. Gall before Christmas, Waldo."

28

South

Ten days after the donation of the two churches, Waldo, Adelinde, Hildegarde and Warin and their entourage left Seeburg towards Trailfingen on the walk back to St. Gall.

They all stopped at the Satan's head tree carving and placed their hands on the sculpture as Waldo blessed them and asked God to take them safely through the forest to Trailfingen. He couldn't help smiling as he remembered the many travellers who had paused and touched the carved Devil's face before heading into the forest. He recalled Othmar's words about fear and included it in his blessing, saying it out loud so they could all hear it.

"Man's oldest fear is the fear of the unknown, a dread of the dark forest – may the Lord God take us safely through this dark forest."

The Lord did guide them safely to Trailfingen, protecting them from the many dangers that were no doubt lurking among the deep shadows in the trees along the way. When the group reached Trailfingen, they

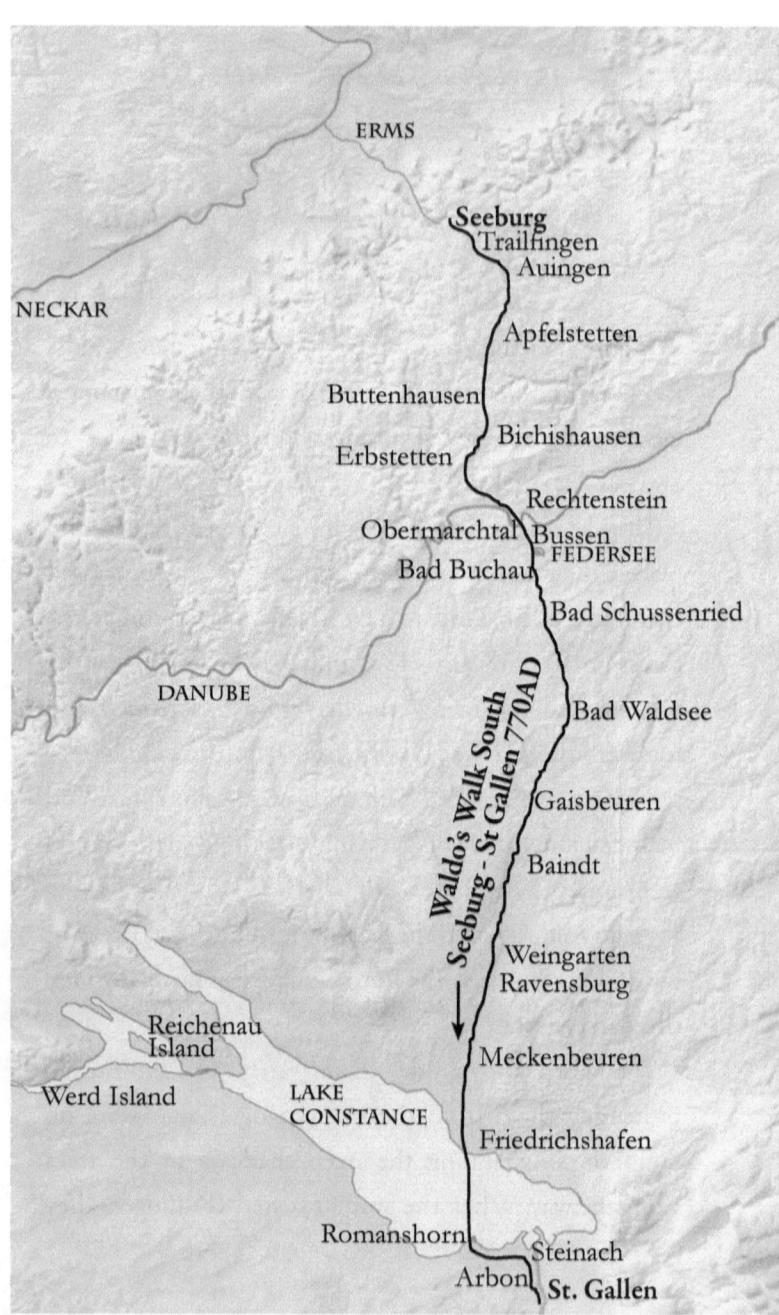

ERMS

Seeburg
Trailfingen
Auingen

NECKAR

Apfelstetten

Buttenhausen
Bichishausen

Erbstetten

Rechtenstein

Obermarchtal Bussen
FEDERSEE

Bad Buchau

Bad Schussenried

DANUBE

Bad Waldsee

Waldo's Walk South
Seeburg - St Gallen 770AD

Gaisbeuren

Baindt

Weingarten
Ravensburg

Reichenau
Island

Meckenbeuren

Werd Island
LAKE
CONSTANCE

Friedrichshafen

Romanshorn
Steinach
Arbon **St. Gallen**

stopped at Waldo's little church there for food and rest. Their timing was perfect because just after they arrived, his local congregation called by and gave them a freshly roasted lamb carcass as a farewell present.

"How generous, God be with all of you!" Waldo said. "We'll eat well tonight my friends!"

"They must have known we were coming," Warin said.

"You are obviously well thought of in your parish, Waldo," Adelinde said. "And you've at least converted those who brought the meat."

They were all hungry and there wasn't much left of the lamb once they'd had their fill.

"We made short work of that!" Waldo said. "There is nothing left but the bones and a few fatty scraps for Zimple." He patted the dog, which was lying at his feet.

After the sun went down the night was cool and still, so everyone sat around a fire close to the church, contentedly digesting their unexpected roast. Suddenly, a breeze swirled briefly past the fire before disappearing into the trees in the darkness beyond the fire's glow. As it reached the trees it wafted through the leaves with a swishing sound, like a long hiss turning into a sigh. It caught everyone's attention and Warin was the first to say what the others were thinking.

"I think we have just been visited by a ghost," he said with a smile, aware of the effect his comment had made on Adelinde and Hildegarde, who huddled nearer the fire.

"No, it couldn't have been a ghost," Waldo said, to the obvious relief of the two women.

Their relief was premature.

"She wouldn't come this far from the graveyard ...," Waldo said thoughtfully, letting his remark hang in the air.

Adelinde and Hildegarde were aghast.

"There is a well known female ghost who regularly appears in the nearby graveyard of Gruorn," Waldo explained earnestly. "It is said she is the spirit of a young girl who died in the Reichenau hospice and walked from there to the Gruorn graveyard. The locals say there is a trail through the forest from Auingen to Gruorn that is known as the Walk of the Dead."

"Well, our ghost wasn't walking," Warin said, "so it wasn't her."

"You're probably right," Waldo agreed.

This didn't help Adelinde and Hildegarde one bit, as they were now faced with the prospect that it was some other ghost that had just swished past them. They were now so close to the fire Waldo feared they would catch alight.

Hildegarde was particularly frightened. She was shivering, despite the heat from the fire, so what Warin said next tipped her over the edge.

"If it is a ghost and it comes back, my sword won't be of any use," he said, holding the weapon up and then jabbing it into the ground next to him.

Hildegarde jumped to her feet with a cry and ran off towards the church, disappearing into the darkness.

Waldo stood up and started to follow her when Adelinde restrained him.

"She will be more terrified if she hears someone coming after her," she said. "Just let her calm down for a short time, and then I will go and talk to her."

Hildegarde didn't get the chance to calm down. Seconds later a terrified scream cut through the night air.

"That's Hildegarde!" Adelinde cried.

Waldo leapt to his feet, grabbed Warin's sword, which was still stuck in the ground, and ran off towards the church where the scream had come from. Warin wasn't far behind him. He pulled a large burning branch out of the fire and ran after Waldo.

Before he saw anything, Waldo heard another scream, followed by a ferocious growl.

There was a dim light reaching the small courtyard from several large candles they had left burning in one of the church windows. Waldo could just make out what was happening. A bear had Hildegarde bailed up against the wall of the church and was swaying to and fro, roaring savagely as it stood over the terrified girl, who had slumped to the ground. Waldo rushed forward, and with all his strength, thrust the sword into the bear's back. The beast howled with pain and rage. It swung round and knocked Waldo off his feet with a single blow of its massive paw. Waldo was sprawled on his back on the ground, but kept his eyes on the bear, and the sword thrust forward. As the enraged animal rushed at Waldo, Warin arrived at a run, waving the burning branch and yelling at the top of his voice.

The bear stopped its attack on Waldo and turned to face Warin. The flames and Warin's shouts momentarily confused the animal, giving Waldo a chance to scramble to his feet. His original thrust with the sword had injured the bear more than he realised, and he could see blood running freely from the wound. With another almighty effort, he thrust the sword into the beast again while it was still distracted by Warin. Waldo felt the blade go deep into the bear's back, and saw the animal shudder.

It staggered briefly as it swung round to face Waldo again. As Waldo backed away the bear stumbled and fell to the ground. With a spine-chilling roar, it regained its feet and lumbered off into the darkness, mortally wounded.

Waldo and Warin stood side-by-side breathing heavily as they stared into the darkness after the bear. Moments later, from deep in the forest, they heard the distant howl of the dying animal.

"God praise your quick thinking," Waldo said to Warin, handing him back his sword. "You saved my life."

"Perhaps," Warin said, "but you definitely saved Hildegarde's life."

The two men thumped each other on the back and turned their attention to Hildegarde. Adelinde was doing her best to comfort her younger sister, who was sobbing uncontrollably.

"Oh Waldo," Adelinde said, with tears streaming down her face, "without you ... our dear Hildegarde ..." Her voice failed her and she buried her face in her sister's trembling shoulder. Waldo crouched down beside her and embraced both women.

A short time later, Adelinde managed to coax Hildegarde to her feet and take her inside the church.

"The bear was after the roast scraps we left out," Waldo said to Warin. "Next time we clean up before we relax by the fire."

†

The group's main destination was the town of Buchau, just south of Lake Federsee. The day after they left Seeburg they visited a miller's wife in Buttenhausen, who over the years supplied flour to Hildegarde's hospice.

Then, after another day's walk, they crossed the Danube near Rechtenstein to Marchtal.

"We aren't far from Lake Federsee," Waldo said. "This is a good place to stop for a rest."

As they made themselves comfortable on fallen logs or grassy patches of ground, Adelinde pointed to a distinctive mountain in the distance that dominated the landscape.

"What is that pointy mountain over there?" she asked Waldo.

"That is the Bussen, the heathens' holy mountain," he said. "It has been visited and revered by the pagans since prehistoric times. It is still a sacred place for their rituals."

Adelinde asked the precise question Waldo hoped she wouldn't.

"What kind of rituals?"

Waldo hesitated because he knew the answer would upset Adelinde, but she was looking at him intensely, silently demanding an answer.

"Up there," he said, nodding his head in the general direction of the mountain, "the pagans sacrifice virgins to their gods so that their women will be fertile."

"Ignorant heathens," said Warin, who was sitting close by. "Paganism is the whore. Christianity is the virgin."

Adelinde didn't react to Warin's remark. She was still coming to terms with what Waldo had said. She didn't gasp or look shocked hearing about virgin sacrifice, but she didn't hide her horror and anger that such barbaric rituals were still taking place. For several hours afterwards, Adelinde was lost in her own thoughts and hardly spoke to anyone. That evening she asked Waldo to come up with a way to stop the virgin sacrifices on the mountain.

Early the next morning in the pre-dawn light, when the Bussen mountain was still a silhouette against the emerging sky, Waldo sat for an hour watching the mountain, hoping it would inspire an idea he could give Adelinde. When she joined him as the sun finally showed itself on the horizon, he smiled at her, confident he had the answer.

"I have invented a legend," he said, "that I will reveal to the pagans, in this way: 'For generations you pagans have sacrificed enslaved girls on top of this mountain. Each time their blood flowed it soaked into the ground, sinking deeper and deeper down into the earth below where it reached a bloodthirsty monster that lives in a cave inside the mountain. But the monster did not feed on the virgins' blood. Instead it turned all the blood into gold and diamonds. Over time it had filled the cave with them and had no more room to breathe. It choked on all the gems and died. So your fertility god cannot help you any longer. He is dead! You must stop sacrificing more virgins. There is a better way to make sure your women are fertile without having to slaughter the innocent young girls. The mother Mary of my Christian God helps infertile women. This has proven to be true not far from here in a small village called Seeburg. At the Christian church in the village there is a wooden statue of this Mary with her faceless infant on her arm. When women who have been unable to have a child stroke the head of the faceless infant and ask my Christian God for a blessing, they become fertile. Send your infertile women to this church at Seeburg and let the young girls of your tribe grow into fertile women themselves.'"

"That is a clever legend you have created, Waldo," Adelinde said. "I think it will help to change the pagans' minds, especially the women's. I'm sure even pagan women will do anything to save the lives of those poor enslaved girls who after all were someones daughters."

She hugged Waldo happily, as she knew full well, that Hildegarde could have been such an enslaved girl some years ago, when her husband and her son lost their lives in the battle at Plankental, not far from here.

"Thank you, dear Waldo," she said.

"I'm not sure Godsbert will thank me when he is

overwhelmed with infertile pagan women at his little church," Waldo said, laughing.

Later that day, the group reached Lake Federsee where Warin's men were to soon start building the monastery for Adelinde and Hildegarde.

Waldo and Warin set to work making preparations, and before long building commenced. Under his personal urging and guidance, Warin's men made rapid progress with the building and seven weeks later Waldo felt confident that the two women would have safe shelter at Lake Federsee.

"The time has come for me to leave, dear Adelinde," he said, embracing her gently.

Neither of them spoke for several minutes, content to let their embrace speak for them. And it had all been said on the walk to Buchau anyway.

Eventually, and reluctantly, they released one another, both physically and emotionally. They stood and admired the magnificent vista, across the reeds where thousands of birds were breeding, to the sparkling water of the lake reflecting the clear blue sky.

"It is so beautiful," Adelinde said, "it must be gazed upon by angels in their flight."

"You are an angel sent to me, by God," Waldo said, "but only temporarily. His plan all along was to send you here to be the first woman abbot of a monastery."

They embraced again.

"This is not a final parting, Adelinde. I will be just three days travel away at St. Gall. You are starting a new monastery and will need support, so there will be reason for me to come and see you occasionally. And remember, I have also promised Charles that I would keep Hildegarde safe."

At dawn the next morning Waldo pushed on south to Lake Constance through Waldsee, Gwigg and Weingarten via St. Veidt to Wasserburg and Buchhorn on the shore of Lake Constance. From there he took a boat across the lake to Arbon. His arduous journey was almost over, the Abbey of St. Gall was just 5 hours away.

At the great gates of the abbey, Waldo paused and thanked God for delivering him back safely. Six years ago he had walked out of these same gates as an eager, newly ordained missionary priest heading north into the pagan barbarian heartland beyond the Danube.

Now he had returned to be a monk in the abbey built on the hermitage site of the holy Irish monk Saint Gall, who was one of the 12 companions of Saint Columbanus who came to this place from Scotland and from Ireland on God's mission more than a century and a half earlier. Waldo was also about to re-enter the abbey whose first abbot was his beloved Othmar.

"I have returned to St. Gall, Othmar," he whispered,

"and so will you."

From the moment he left Adelinde at Lake Federsee, Waldo had been thinking about how he could secretly remove Othmar's remains from Werd Island and return it to St. Gall. It was already late August so he knew he would have to do it soon, before winter arrived.

†

To his surprise and delight, Waldo found that his two friends from the final training days at the abbey and the walk north, Jonas and Theo, were also back at St. Gall. Both had returned more than a year earlier and were already well established as monks.

"We have some stories to share," Waldo said as the three friends met in the cloister one crisp autumn morning. "But first I have a favour to ask. It is more important to me than anything I have done in the past six years."

Theo and Jonas didn't hesitate for a moment to agree to join Waldo's secret mission to bring Othmar's remains back to St. Gall.

"There are several other monks here," Jonas said, "who would also be willing to come with us, I'm sure."

"We will need the abbot's permission," Waldo said. "I will have to invoke the power of a higher authority, I think."

"You mean boast about your powerful friends," Jonas said with a grin.

"Exactly," Waldo replied. "King Charles is coming here before Christmas, mainly to see me, so perhaps the abbot will not feel inclined to say no to the king's dear friend, the humble monk, Waldo."

The abbot of St. Gall listened attentively to Waldo's request, then nodded.

"The most holy Othmar, the first abbot of this great abbey, belongs here," he said solemnly. "Go and bring him back to us, Waldo, with my blessing, in the sight of the Lord God."

Ten nights later Waldo stood with Theo and Jonas, and two other monks, on the shore of Lake Constance, where it empties into the river Rhine, looking out across the water to Werd Island, just a dim shape in the darkness. He might have imagined it, but he was certain he felt a twinge in his jaw that recalled the beating he had suffered at the hands of Ruthard on that same spot many years before. He blocked such unhappy thoughts from his mind and concentrated on the task at hand.

"I have found out the location of Othmar's grave," Waldo said. "It is marked by a white cross. A priest from Steinach took it upon himself to give Othmar a dignified burial, and he has been tending the grave every few months. I have met him and told him our plans. It is to his church that we will first take Othmar's remains by boat and prepare them for travel to St. Gall. He will have a horse and cart ready for us on the shore at Steinach."

Rowing out to the island, Waldo was suddenly back there on the night he left the food for Othmar hanging on the tree in the torchlight.

"No torches," he said. "We'll complete our mission in the dark." Once again it occurred to him that Charles would love to be there with them.

This time there were no unseen observers waiting on the shore to beat him senseless. There was only the priest standing silently in the darkness with the horse and cart as he had promised.

The next evening, the cart carried Othmar's remains through the gates of St. Gall Abbey, accompanied by the celestial sound of monks chanting prayers.

"Waldo," Jonas said in a hushed voice. "The small barrel of wine the priest at Steinach gave us ... it's still full."

"Admirable abstinence shown by all," Waldo replied, grinning. "We'll drink it later to celebrate our successful mission."

"Waldo, we have been drinking it ... all of us. You had a cup or two as well."

"And it's still full?" Waldo asked.

Jonas nodded.

"Praise the Lord," Waldo said. "It is a sign that in God's eyes, Othmar is already a Saint. And Othmar would be delighted with such a sign – he was known to enjoy the nectar of the vineyard."

"Perhaps the Lord God has a sense of humour," Jonas said with a quiet chuckle.

"He needs one," Waldo said. "We test His love and patience relentlessly."

Just as we tested your love and patience, dear Othmar, Waldo said to himself. And then we sent you away to die a long and lonely death. But the good Lord didn't forsake you. And now He has delivered you home.

That evening the abbey bells rang out to the heavens that Othmar, its first abbot was back in the bosom of St. Gall. Waldo stood at the grave the monks had dug in the centre of the herb garden, first planted by Othmar, and said farewell. The abbot had allowed Waldo the honour of throwing the first sod of earth into the grave. He scooped it up with both hands and dropped it on the pine coffin at the bottom of the hole.

He held back a small amount and placed it in a leather pouch. I'll save it for Charles, he thought. He can also throw the first sod on Othmar's grave when he gets here.

29

Sin

Waldo could hear Othmar's voice clearly in his mind.

"Now, you must listen very carefully boys. Many herbs are from God's own garden. They are a wonderful medicine that can ease terrible pain and save countless lives. But the Devil himself also has a small, secret herb garden of his own. As you would expect, his herbs work in the completely opposite way that God's do."

Waldo stood with Charles in the herb garden at St. Gall as his friend threw the small amount of earth he had saved for him, onto Othmar's grave. He had remembered Othmar's instructions about God's herbs and the Devil's herbs word for word, and had just recited them to Charles as they walked through the herb garden to the grave.

"I remember him talking about God's herbs and the Devil's herbs," Charles said, gazing into the distance.

Waldo was gazing into some hidden recesses of his own mind.

"The secret herbs from the Devil's garden are not to be found here." he said. "They grow wild in a hidden part of the forest not far from here. I know where to find them.

We can go together and collect some."

The friends were finding it difficult to look one another in the eye. A tense silence prevailed while each examined his conscience.

As befits a warrior king, Charles was the first to crash through the barrier.

"It must be done," he said. "Otherwise my brother will destroy the empire, and Christendom with it ... everything our father and grandfather fought their whole lives for. There is no other way."

Charles was looking directly at Waldo, who had chosen the abbey bell tower to look at. He was staring at it so intensely it seemed he was trying to make the bell ring by sheer force of will. He could feel Charles's eyes on him and finally relented, meeting his gaze.

"Yes, it must be done," he said, firmly. "I just wish the method wasn't something dear Othmar had taught us."

†

The next day Waldo and Charles rode north, following the river along the valley to the forest several hours away. Waldo had been a good rider as a boy and had tried hard to maintain some degree of horse riding skill during his six years at Seeburg.

And of course Charles was keen to test him out and

insisted on a race at full gallop. Waldo was chasing Charles more than racing him, but he was surprised at how well he handled the horse, and was exhilarated by the wild ride.

"Ah, Waldo!" Charles sang out as he turned and waited for Waldo to catch up. "Just like we used to race those ponies along the Breisgau as boys!"

They gave the horses time to recover and sat in silence, simply enjoying the fresh air and one another's company.

Charles suddenly pointed skyward without breaking the silence. Waldo looked up to see two great eagles locked in mortal combat. Their talons were hooked together and they were spinning wildly, spiralling rapidly towards the forest below.

As Charles and Waldo watched mesmerised by the sight, the two birds crashed down through the forest canopy and disappeared into the trees. Moments later one of the eagles reappeared, thrashing its wings clear of the branches before flying off towards a line of distant hills. The men waited for several minutes, but there was no sign of the second eagle.

"I have heard of eagles spinning and spiralling out of the sky," Charles said, "but I have never witnessed it before."

"Incredible," Waldo said.

"I don't want to sound mystical or superstitious," Charles said, "but it may be a sign. So, I hope the eagle that emerged from the forest was me."

"You don't believe in omens, do you Charles?"

"No, omens are pagan beliefs. But I do believe in the power of symbolism to give one inspiration and strength. Let's keep riding and find that hidden bit of forest."

It wasn't hard to find. Waldo knew precisely where the deadly herbs grew. After another hour's ride, he called a halt, and dismounted. He walked his horse along a narrow piece of ground between huge boulders on one side and thick forest on the other. The trees and rocks formed a natural alleyway that gradually grew narrower and darker until both sides met.

Waldo pointed at a dense, tangled mass of vegetation and purple-blue flowers growing over boulders, through tree roots and up the trunks.

"This even feels like an evil place," Charles said. "A devil's lair."

"We don't need much," Waldo said, resisting the temptation to bless himself. "Let's collect it and go."

Charles broke off a small stem: "What is it?"

"Othmar called it Devilshood. You were right when you called this place a devil's lair."

Waldo had filled a small sack with Devilshood and was eager to leave. They walked their horses back through the natural alleyway of forest and boulders.

"I have tried everything in my power to make peace with Carloman, for Bertrada's sake," Charles said. "But he is resolute. I have even tried to meet with him, but he refuses to see me. I saw Bertrada in Seeburg after you left. He told her he will see me dead, or die trying. And so he will."

He shut his eyes briefly, as if he was trying to recover a lost thought.

"If Carloman and I go to war, many men will die. Carolingian, Christian men. Men who should be brothers – "

Charles's voice died in his throat momentarily, but he recovered quickly.

"Carolingian, Christian men should be brothers-in-arms, not mortal enemies. Carloman is not interested in protecting our father's empire or Christianity, he is just interested in being the king, by himself ... even if it destroys the Carolingian dynasty."

As they mounted their horses to begin the journey back to St. Gall, Charles grasped Waldo's arm.

"We do this thing in God's name," Waldo. "We sin for God. He will forgive us."

"But can we forgive ourselves, Charles?"

"We must, Waldo. If God forgives us, who are we to defy His will? He has appointed you and me to build and defend Christianity. We are both soldiers in God's army going into battle against the pagans. You walk, I march."

Waldo put his hands together in prayer.

"We are the cross and the sword," he said.

Charles slammed his fist into his hand.

"Our will be done!"

"Amen," Waldo said softly.

†

Carloman died on December 4, 771AD at the Villa of Samoussy after a long illness, apparently of natural causes, a severe nosebleed is claimed as being at fault. Drinking any amount of herbal infusions couldn't save him.

Epilogue by Godsbert

My garden is most beautiful at this gentle time of the day. The softening sun deepens the hue of every flower and enriches the birdsong. Even though I have been a Christian all my life, to me the sun is still a god. It provides the energy for life and nurtures the earth and every creature that walks upon it and flies above it.

Many years ago I stood here in this very spot, when the garden was just a rough plan in my head, and half-jokingly suggested to my beloved master, Father Waldo, that I should carve a tree stump in his likeness. "I think a likeness of a saint would be more appropriate, Godsbert," my master had said sternly.

But I think in his heart he was secretly pleased with the idea. In my eyes he is now a Saint anyway, no matter what the Pope and his pompous cardinals might think. And so my statue of Waldo stands in my garden, a full length, life-size image of him carved in wood with his feet firmly rooted in the sacred soil of Seeburg.

He is standing in his favourite spot near the river admiring the little octagon Church of the Holy Mary that we had just finished building. Waldo has his arms outstretched, his face joyous, as if saying to the world, "Behold our tiny church, is it not as magnificent as the most splendid cathedral in the land!" He is holding a hammer in one hand. It is the actual hammer he was using on that final day of building, which I have made part of the statue.

The local blacksmith has worked a small iron plate that I have fixed to the bottom of the statue. Etched in the metal are the words, *Here stands Waldo of Seeburg who became Imperial Bishop of the Carolingian Empire. 741-814.* He would be happy to know that the blacksmith who made the plate was the son of the man who made our first church bell in 765.

It was a few years ago that I made the statue. But it was my last because I lost the spirit to carve after that. And I am now too old and frail to hold the chisel firmly and drive the hammer hard enough. The year I carved the tree stump in Waldo's likeness was 814 and I had just heard of my sainted master's passing. I think of him as Waldo of Seeburg. Although he had many far grander titles in his extraordinary lifetime, I don't think any would please him more than *Waldo of Seeburg*.

From the day Waldo left me to take over from him in Seeburg in 770, until his death in 814, I diligently followed his progress and achievements whenever possible, and wrote down every scrap of information about him that I came in possession of. I also tried to record everything I could about the life and times of his friend and master, King Charles - Charlemagne.

Father Waldo went from here in 770 to the Cloister of St. Gall to become a Benedictine monk, arriving there in August of that year.

A fellow monk of his, Brother Jonas came through Seeburg the following year. I remembered him as one of Waldo's travelling companions when we all first walked north from Reichenau Abbey in 764.

Jonas told me that Waldo made a rapid success of himself at St. Gall and soon after arriving became a deacon and talented scribe. He was always a wonderful writer and it is only through his patient tutoring that I am able to write the words you are reading now.

I don't think it is coincidence that after Waldo's arrival, St. Gall would be one of the first abbeys to install glass windows and heated rooms for the scribes to make bearable their long hours of reading and writing. He was always of a practical mind and would devote a great deal of time thinking about better ways to do things. However, he never did come up with a device to simplify the writing process.

He once remarked that even though one was seated while writing, and that just one hand was used to manipulate a small, light instrument, it was a most tiring pursuit. He would occasionally say to me, "Godsbert, even if only three fingers are holding the pen, the whole body is involved in the writing process."

My task of making a thorough record of Waldo and Charlemagne's activities after 770 Anno Domini would have been impossible if it had not been for a wonderful stroke of good fortune.

Up until 781, Waldo had been keeping a record of significant dates and events in his life in a diary. By then he was the Abbot of Reichenau, and the monastery had flourished under his leadership.

In that year of 781 Charlemagne met Pope Hadrian I in Rome and promised he would stabilise Lombardy by making his son Pippin the child king based in Pavia.

He also sent Waldo to Pavia as the boy's guardian and to administer the dioceses of Pavia and Bâle.

Before he left Reichenau, Waldo gave his diary to a close friend and confidant, Brother Theo, who was also on our original walk north. He asked Theo that if he was ever in the region of Seeburg to deliver it to me. The next year the good Lord sent Theo through Seeburg and I took possession of Waldo's precious diary.

It was the year 782 and it turned out to be one of deep misgiving for Waldo, and of great ignominy for his dear friend King Charlemagne. The king had been grievously offended by a Saxon uprising and in retribution had ordered the decapitation of 4,500 unarmed pagan nobles in a bloodbath at a place called Verden on the river Aller.

At this point in my writings it seems sensible to revert to

the entries in Waldo's diary. However, they contain many musings and remarks of a personal nature for Waldo, which without his blessing, I am reluctant to reveal.

So I will simply convey the factual information of the events concerned and not intrude on the innermost thoughts and emotions of my beloved master. The diary entries begin in 771, the year after Waldo left Seeburg.

771 AD

A momentous year for both Charlemagne and Waldo. The king divorced his Lombardian wife Desiderata and sent her back to her father in Pavia. Desiderius was not happy and determined to make life difficult for Charlemagne at every opportunity thereafter.

Later that year, Charlemagne married Hildegarde in a secret ceremony in Buchau at Lake Federsee, with Waldo by his side.

It is not mentioned by Waldo in his diary, but I know that Charlemagne's brother Carloman died suddenly in December 771 at the Villa of Samoussy from uncertain causes. Some say he died of natural causes as the result of a severe nosebleed. Others say he was deliberately poisoned. They say a nosebleed of such severity, must have been caused by a powerful herb that he unknowingly ingested in his food or herbal tea.

On his brother's death, Charlemagne acted swiftly and

sent Carloman's wife Gerberga back to her father King Desiderius in Lombardy. He did so to prevent Gerberga from claiming any Frankish land rights for her one-year old son as inheritance from his father Carloman.

What happened next was a shock to me, I must admit, and I agonised over revealing it. However, I discovered that it is already known to certain monks at St. Gall and Reichenau and I could see no point in trying to hide it. And it is not for me to judge that Waldo would want it hidden anyway.

When Charlemagne ordered Gerberga's banishment from the empire she travelled to St. Gall to ask Waldo for his advice as to what she should do.

The two briefly fell in love and Waldo sired a child – it was his only ever child as far as I now. It was a girl, later named Ida, who grew up as a foster child with a noble family in Pavia at town in Lombardy where Waldo became Bishop and guardian of Charlemagne's son.

It seems Charlemagne knew about Waldo's illegitimate daughter and personally arranged her placement with the noble family and her marriage to Count Ekbert of Herzfeld.

772 AD

Hildegarde has her first of eight children with Charlemagne. It's a boy called Charles, like his father.

773 AD

Hildegarde has a second child, a girl called Adelhaid, named after Charlemagne's sister who died at birth.

774 AD

Charlemagne wins a war against his former father-in-law Desiderius. He banishes the Lombardy king and his family to a monastery and declares himself King of the Lombards.

775 AD

Hildegarde has yet another daughter called Rotrud, named after Charlemagne's grandmother. This year Charlemagne starts a war against the Saxons.

776 AD

Charlemagne crosses the Alps to quash a revolt by the Lombardians.

777 AD

Here I found my own name written in my beloved Waldo's hand and the tears flowed freely for some time. I was overcome with both happiness that he came into my life, and grief that he is gone. But soon, the Lord God willing, I will be with him in heaven.

Waldo's entry reads, *On October 12, 777AD, Godsbert*

donated the octagon church at Seeburg to the cloister Lorsch.

Also in this same year, Hildegarde has a second son, who they first called Carlomann but for obvious reasons renamed him Pippin after Charles's father.

781 AD

Charlemagne sent Waldo as bishop to Pavia, to become the guardian of Charlemagne's second son Pippin, the child king of the Lombardy.

786 AD

Waldo became Abbot of Reichenau Abbey, where he established a library, a school and a herb garden.

800 AD

At Mass, on Christmas Day (25 December), when Charlemagne knelt at the altar to pray, the Pope Leo II crowned him Imperator Romanorum ("Emperor of the Romans") in Saint Peter's Basilica.

802 AD

Perhaps here I can add a whimsical note: Charlemagne had been gifted an elephant called Abul-Abbas, by the caliph of Baghdad, Harun al-Rashid. On July 1, 802, the elephant arrived at Aachen, also known as Aix-la-

Chapelle, Charlemagne's favourite residence.

Here, as he promised Hildegarde, Charlemagne built an octagon church dedicated to Saint Mary. It was like a replica of our octagon church in Seeburg only much bigger and out of stone of course. He even replicated my timber 'throne', what an honour.

805 AD

Charlemagne made Waldo his Imperial Abbot and Abbot of the Carolingian Abbey of St. Denis near Paris.

814 AD

On January 28, 814, Charlemagne, Carolus Rex, died in Aachen and was buried in a secret spot in his octagon church. He once mentioned to Waldo, that his greatest wish was, that his mortal body would never be found, so history could claim his resurection from the dead.

The monks in Aachen exclaimed:

"From the lands where the sun rises to western shores, people are crying and wailing... the Franks, the Romans, all Christians, are stung with mourning and great worry... the young and old, glorious nobles, all lament the loss of their Caesar... the world laments the death of Charles the Great... O Christ, you who governs the heavenly host, grant a peaceful place to mighty Charles in your everlasting kingdom."

814 AD

On Saturday, May 27 of the same year, my beloved mentor Waldo died and entered the kingdom of heaven where the Almighty welcomed one of his holiest sons.

In farewell, the monks declared:

"You will never be forgotten in this place. As long as this fleeting world exists, your name will be endlessly praised, Waldo, oh thou most holy man."

†

I am *Godsbert of Seeburg* in Alemannia in autumn of this year of our Lord 817.

Postscript

So ended Godsbert's record of certain significant events that occurred after Waldo left him at Seeburg in 770AD and departed for St. Gall.

Waldo rested in peace for over 1,000 years, largely forgotten or suppressed by the Roman Catholic Church.

Then in 1858 his memory was revived by the Protestant pastor Heber, who wrote an historical study about Waldo called *The True Protestant*. In it he attempts to prove that *Waldo of Reichenau*, the Christian adviser of Charlemagne, was in fact *the first Protestant*, predating Martin Luther by more than 700 years.

In 2002, the town of Seeburg published a book about its history. It contained a photograph of an existing document recording Waldo's donation to the cloister Lorsch of churches in Seeburg, Trailfingen and Auingen, plus some meadows.

In 2012, intrigued by the age old donation document, Klaus D Wagner began to research Waldo's history and legacy. His findings inspired him to write the historic novel '*Waldo*' that you now hold in your hands.

It is followed by the historic novels '*Godsbert*' and '*Carolus*' to conclude the '*Charlemagne Trilogy*'.

Epiphany

As long as we remember them,
they will never die.

The Charlemagne Trilogy Volume II

Godsbert
Charlemagne's Scribe

Klaus D Wagner

Charlemagne and his childhood friend Waldo, promoted Godsbert to become one of their favourite scribes, not only to copy the Holy Scriptures, but to write a hagiography of their favourite teacher Othmar, who was the first Abbot of St. Gall, a Benedictine monastery in the early Middle Ages.

The pious Othmar lived a life of holy work and miracles, but was doomed to a tragic fate.

Read the second book of the Charlemagne Trilogy.

The Charlemagne Trilogy Volume III

Carolus
Charlemagne's Life

Klaus D. Wagner

Charlemagne was obsessed with how history would judge and portray him. One of his greatest desires was to be counted among the just.

He asked his childhood friend and Imperial Abbot Waldo, to find the scribe who could best set his atrocities, committed against the medieval pagans, in a good light.

But did he succeed?

Read about the historic, mythical resurrection of Charlemagne's life in this intriguing trilogy.

9 783740 708962